FREAKS AND FEMALES

STORIES THAT SHOULDN'T BE SHARED.

ZOE ROSE

CONTENTS

For Steve, whose stories were better than anything I could ever write—especially the ones I wasn't supposed to hear. And for his partner, Tim, who has joined with him once more.

For Maw, who was too sweet to read something like this. If Heaven has a library, I hope you aren't too shocked by what your great-grandbaby's been writing.

ADAM AND EVE IN QUARANTINE

S unday. Sunny Day. Adam makes coffee. Eve makes turmeric tea. She saw it on Instagram. She's seen a lot about it lately.

Turmeric is apparently one of those magical anti-inflammatories that can do everything: clears skin, burns belly fat, boosts sex drive, and gives a kick without caffeine. Boosts the immunity, too. Eve knows it's no true panacea, but it certainly couldn't hurt, especially when it was a deal on Prime.

She sent the post to Adam, but if he ever opened it she doesn't know. He didn't reply and she doesn't want to *be annoying but* ask him about it, especially if his silence was the response after all. They sit on their respective ends of the couch, sipping their drinks without commentary.

Instead Eve opens her mouth to mention the snakes she'd dreamt of last night, of a river come alive with cottonmouths, but then thinks better of it. She knows exactly how it would go: if he doesn't just give a caveman grunt in response, he will ask what her point in sharing that was. And she wouldn't have one, not one he'd accept without any followup questions. And it'd either start something or nothing for the rest of their Sunday morning and probably carry on over into the night, and Eve doesn't know which outcome she'd prefer at this point.

A little noise, *pff*, escapes when she puts her lips back together. She isn't going to waste her breath. Not now.

Just as she feels the urge to shit—finally, frankly—

Adam gets up and shuts himself in the bathroom. Eve bites back the *are you kidding me* and instead reaches for her paperback on the coffee table. It would be a while.

By the time he's come out again, Eve has no more of the *natural momentum* she's so delicately explained to him so many god damn times. If she doesn't go when she needs to go, when won't be going at all.

He goes whenever—and all the time, apparently. Eve wonders whether his phone can track how many hours he spends in there the way it tracks steps and screen time and sleep. Eve also knows that no number would shock him into any real revelation.

She's tried timing him before to *make a point* and it only pissed him off. Now she doesn't even bother checking the time when he goes in, so there's no telling how long he'd been in there today. At least long enough for her to be surprised that it's already 10 AM, but then again, it's been increasingly easy to lose all sense of time.

Lately, an hour equals a day and also a minute all at once. It's given Eve perspective, though, of what it must be like to have ADHD. Or serve time in solitary. Or to be in Purgatory. It's all very interesting when she can think about it at arm's length.

Eve's read that women experience time differently even in the most normal conditions and that it can further vary between cultures. Adam and Eve are of the same background—Eve was raised that way, anyhow—but of course there lay the matter of sex, organ differences that let them join together in at least one way, sometimes. This time, not a word between them as she turns in her shoulders to pass him in the hallway.

She almost bothers to joke that he could have the bathroom all day at this point, to *sit on the toilet and watch porn until your ass goes numb* or whatever it is he does in there. This little dig—she knows it's a dig, isn't anything other than a dig—stays unsaid.

Eve still gets shy about bringing up her *bathroom particularities* to her own doctor and she cried when she had to tell Adam about why she *wasn't trying to be a control freak but it's literally one chance in the morning or not at all*. Now, though, she doesn't give a shit. Chronic manmade constipation will have even the old dame of an etiquette school plainly state her need to poop without so much as a stutter.

She has no use for the bathroom now, not even for doing her makeup or hair. She'll have to wait a minute —there's an almost evil smell emanating from there that has her moving along, moving along past that door.

So off Eve goes to the bedroom to change into her new ($56.32) workout set. It's pink, maybe more pink than she would've wanted. It didn't look like this online. On the screen it seemed more muted, less look-at-me and more my-life-is-organized-enough-to-have-coordinated-athletic-wear. That's what Eve had been going for, anyway.

But Eve is fighting hard against the COVID Nineteen, and she tells herself it's like dressing for the job you want but instead of a job, it's her body. Not that there's any real issue with her weight or self-confidence. She is not unhappy with herself. When she looks at the 20-something brunette with small breasts and big eyes, she is more or less fine with what she sees. Really.

But she doesn't want to waste time, not when they have been given so much of it. Eternity can only go so long and Eve wants something to show for it, for whenever this all ends. Isolation to transformation— Eve wants nothing more than to be changed, but she must do it to herself.

Eve will not go back to work in the same shameful state as everyone else: double-chinned, blanched from too much screen time, bent at the neck. Eve will emerge from lockdown like any animal that cyclically goes away and comes back new. Better. Too attractive to be overlooked. And this shade, bright and screamingly feminine, forces her into focus. *I am here, I am fucking here, someone please take note.* It is not so much a prayer as it is an affirmation. Or vice versa.

It's really not too bad, the color. That pink-pink-pink shade stretched against her body isn't washing her out like she worried. Her complexion has actually gotten so much better since they've left the office. It still surprises her, how sun-loved she looks when she walks by the mirror. Eve feels like she's much paler than that. But maybe those subliminals are actually working.

She ordered the set two weeks ago in what you might call an "aspirational size" and it fits, if a bit snugly. Eve wouldn't wear this in regular life, but she has to remind herself that there's no one to look at her and her too-tight clothes. Run like nobody's watching, or whatever. She rarely even sees a dog walker when she's out there. In what her world has shrunk down to, Eve is effectively the only woman left.

Empty world or not, she still pulls on the band of her sports bra so it doesn't make little fat bulges underneath her shoulders and picks at her leggings until there's just enough strategic wrinkles in the fabric to de-emphasize her admittedly unsatisfactory thighs. She glances over in the mirror on the door, makes a quick assessment of her bloated stomach, and slips on a white workout tank that goes all the way down to where her legs split in two. Then, she goes outside.

Sundays are for self care. At least that's what Eve's been reading—you have to take a day to prioritize yourself, or else it'll never happen. It doesn't take much to start slipping and especially when everyone is wearing sweatpants below their webcams and forgoing deodorant, upkeep has to be codified into a routine. So, Sundays.

Sundays are for sheet masks and shaving and showers until the water runs cold. For healthy meal preps and hair treatments and heavy moisturizers that leave every inch so smooth, so fuckable, even if Adam is always somehow exhausted and she *doesn't want to get into it so just go to bed then*.

Eve doesn't rest on Sundays, though. She likes to start her week by getting a 5k run out of her way. It's like, if she can do this much before Monday, then she can make it through another week. And if she can make it through another week, then she can choose a couple things in the virtual cart she fills up during Zoom meetings. It's a carrot-and-stick way to live, minus the stick.

She starts at a brisk walk down their driveway, picking up the pace every couple of steps. She reaches a steady jog by the time she can't see where she came from. Each block she puts between herself and the house has her feeling lighter, like she's running on the moon. She's nearly sprinting when she reaches where the paved sidewalk turns into a wooded trail, but it's a speed she can sustain. Eve could go on like this forever.

All it is is exercise, though—endorphins don't come to her like everyone else. The "runner's high" she hears of only happens a little bit, maybe, when she's doing the cool down walk back home, and they're gone by the time she's getting out her keys at the door. She hopes she's just doing something wrong, that one day she'll get it right and get closed-hand hit with it.

She wouldn't mind if it hurt a little bit the way an expensive massage does, when they work out a knot and the pain is like productive. She wouldn't mind if something else happened, either. She recently saw a daytime talkshow where they talked about that— something about thighs rubbing together in a rhythm and the beat of feet against a hard surface, you know. But not even the toy she hides behind cleaning supplies in the bathroom can do that for her lately.

She tries to feel the warmth of the Florida sunshine on her skin, the light breeze getting under her tank top, the bright green treetops blurring by in her peripheral. But she only experiences this moment like someone watching a movie. The girl going down the path is another Eve entirely.

Other Eve is enjoying the embrace of nature as she outruns her sexual frustration. Other Eve is wearing this overpriced workout set and attracting the occasional honk from a horny driver. Other Eve has a bed frame and multiple pairs of shoes and A/C and dinner already prepared and more than she had as a kid or could ever ask for now. Other Eve is drowning in her own privilege. Other Eve is really a charmed, charmed girl.

And where is she?

Eve is grateful they got their starter home so close to a state park, she will say that much. If they had to do this lockdown in the old downtown apartment, she absolutely would have smothered Adam in his sleep by now. At least now she has somewhere to go when the four walls start to close in on her. That is a blessing she must always count.

Fuck—someone up ahead. The figure becomes familiar as the distance shortens. A familiar stranger, anyway. Eve has seen her coming in and out of the house next door. Swimming in the pool out back. Once, she saw her walking topless by the kitchen window. Eve has seen the girl go on her own runs and when she sees her leave for one, Eve will wait until she sees her come back. That's when she'll kill the time by going to the bathroom—if Adam isn't there. But now here they are.

The neighbor girl is clearly going to pass by and so

Eve stops to pull a sweaty mask out of the pocket in her waistband. The girl, today in a tight snakeprint one-piece, starts slowing her pace before stopping what Eve has to assume is about six feet away. Eve hooks one loop over her ear, but the girl holds up her hand.

"I don't think you got any cooties," she says. She's got that low-pitched, smoothy-slow way of talking that makes Eve listen. And Eve obeys. It's one of those single-use disposables that Eve has probably worn too many times to be effective, anyways. She puts it back in her pocket. The girl smiles. "I'm just so fucking tired of all this, aren't you?"

Eve's not sure why she does, but she nods. It feels like there's a stone in her throat. The girl takes a step closer.

"I don't think we've ever met," she says. "I mean, I've seen you jogging the same way so many times, but...well, I guess especially right now we should know thy neighbor and all that...my name is Lilly."

"Eve," she finally gasps, "and you're the first person I've spoken to in three days."

This is all too fast, much too fast, but it's exactly right. Lilly has a mean smile and the tell-tale bumps of a pierced nipple poking out from her spandex. It's obvious she knows exactly what she's doing, that she knows who Eve is and what she needs. It took less than a minute to crack, and maybe that's the productive pain Eve wanted after all. The hurts-so-good of losing control.

And it feels *so* fucking good—someone looking at her, responding to her words, acknowledging her existence. And honestly, nobody has looked at her like that —whatever that is—in forever. Eve is seen. Isolation to transformation to selection. So when Lilly offers to show her a little-used trail that takes them to a spring, Eve is only all too happy to follow.

And that, yes, is exactly how she blows her life up.

WHEN VANITY IS OTHERWISE THE POOR GIRL'S ONLY VIRTUE.

They own every breath that we take.
They pick each piece off our plate.
They run the whole of our fate.
And they say it's all for our sake.

— WHAT WE ARE NOT SUPPOSED
TO SING EXCEPT WHEN WE ARE
ALONE.

We've all heard, for quite some time of course, about our master's first tragic passion. There'd been many more little dears who had died off before their faces could crease: three in fruitless childbirth, two by consumption, the one malbred girl he had delivered to the Gods for the lovers she kept when he was away. They'd all been mourned, yes, but in time they are all quietly shaken off to welcome the next girl we would call Lady Nigh.

But then there always remains that stain of the first. Though she had never made it to set foot in this palace, in this land of revolving draperies and cast-aside eyes, her presence clings like an odor. The never-heard, never-seen spirit echoes in the chambers that should've been filled to the brim with heirs made by her blood, kept noisy by her songs that our master will still mumble.

The others that arrived after Her had all came and lived and lived no more, their journeys played out, but this was that Blessed Creature who should've been. Time, the constant unceasing years, and all that was left up to Her supposed life unrealized has smoothed her memory into something perfect and worshiped and too wondrous for any pitiful coming wife to uphold.

For the girls like me, the sealed-mouth servants who run about to keep up this gilded world, the First Lady offers up a certain kind of hope. When we are handed our paltry wages at the end of every week, we think: *The First Lady would have had us paid much better.* When we are slapped by the current wife—usually a pale-lipped girl not much older than ourselves—for pulling her dress in too tight or some other slight offense, we think: *The First Lady never would have raised her hand at us.* When we have our hair yanked and pared off at the end of each month per his orders, we think: *The First Lady would have allowed us keep our locks as long as hers.*

And when the master throws the oldest of us to his miscreant workmen, to the ones who aren't good enough to find a wife on their own, we think: *Should the First Lady have come and shown him what love really is, we would never have our hands forced to these unions.* There is not one thing done to us that she would not have done better. And because she never did anything to us at all, she will remain perfect—to everyone. But especially to us.

The First Lady, as I said, never came to prove our dreams wrong, and so she stays as the secret saint among us laboring maidens. And like every saintly and venerated thing, she had been struck down by a tragedy whispered to us in the quiet before sleep by our mothers and repeated back to our very own new-made daughters who'll once again carry these words after we've rejoined the creators who rest in the cool ground.

Listen. Between me and a few of the other reading girls, we've managed to put down the tragics eternally here. The paper robs the story of its sort of breathless, illicit quality that has drawn us to it, to her, but yet it remains—

Once upon a time—not yet long enough ago to be ancient, but another time indeed. In another land, a land at once unreachably far but not unbearably foreign, lived a king and queen who enjoyed all the luxuries of life entitled to our royals except for one: a child.

What would be but a simple domestic tragedy for commoners, this predicament is dangerous for those who rule the lands. The queen's barren womb could have caused a war, had she not finally fallen pregnant when she did. What she did not say was what it took to make her a mother; the many medicine women she met in the dark stayed there.

Maybe it was these less-than-illustrious actions that led to the tragedy. The Gods do not look kindly upon those who force life, not even the very Godliest of us. This is never to be repeated outside our own shacks, but our kings and queens and ladies and lords? They may do with us as they like, but they are capped under the same sky. All men must answer to the Gods, and Their justice is dealt with an unforgiving hand.

And it was dealt like a double-edged sword. The First Lady was a girl born so beautiful and so pure that she was stolen away the very same night of her birth by a crooked old woman who tried to pull from her those illustrious qualities as one would a tapestry by a thread.

But unravel her the old woman could not, and the girl managed to etch out a passably happy existence within the confines of a high tower built right in a thicket of the woods nearest our own kingdom, for she had been spirited far, far from the home she had been born to. Her upbringing in captivity was spent practicing songs she knew, somehow, from the womb of which she came, and brushing and plaiting her rich, shining hair as it continue to grow and grow and grow.

By the time our master—then but the boyish heir of the titan before him—happened upon her traces while hunting, she had passed enough years there that her voice could carry clear and lovely across the air for miles, miles that our would-be-will-be master had tracked with the hunger of a starving animal. Forbidden by the old woman to cut her hair, scissors being so good at cutting old throats and all, the girl's braid was long enough to swing teasingly within his reach once the master finally made it to her prison of heights.

It was, as he may've confessed to somebody or maybe just to the Gods, the truest pang he'd ever felt for a pretty-faced girl. He was, of course, used to such delights that the courtesans of our land could offer, and even by his early age he could no longer be swayed by such superficial charms. He was immune to shimmery things, yes, but her beauty was backed by other, more ethereal qualities—her curved and plump mouth held within it a clever tongue, the girl's hands were as girlishly smooth as they were crafty and nimble, and she possessed a pair of emerald eyes that could determine everything in a only single glance.

And when those emerald eyes locked down with the pleading ones that squinted up at her peak, her singing abruptly stopped, the sudden silence hanging thick in their atmosphere. He squirmed under her gaze, yet he would not break it. After some time, she finally gave him a smile with the warmth of the sun meeting skin, and began to sing once more—a love song. He knew.

There were many nights where he would slip away from his public, nights he'd ride the miles to again catch her songs. And that was *just* to catch her songs, sometimes another smile. To inhale the sweet, blossom perfume she emanated from above. She was his heaven, and he was her duly pilgrim. Theirs was a chaste love, a courtship only royal women could receive. He never asked to come up. He would never wish to disgrace her like that.

But there came that night she threw down her hair so that he may enter her realm and adore her every detail. So that he could press his lips against hers and declare everything past the horizon of trees to be truly at her feet. To at last plot her escape, their wild chance to bear past the concrete walls and bring her forth to all the courts and lords and ladies and artists and fools and a king and queen that'll just love her, love her too, love her at least half as much as he…

After a slow descent by her own braid, the girl took unsteadily to her bare feet. She'd never felt the ground before, never been underneath the sky. She spent some moments with her arms stretched toward the air as she made a wordless blessing to the stars that'd guide them and the horse that would take them there.

But the horse—

That's when they made the cold discovery that the horse had run off, its bondage to a young tree having been freshly cut. With a sick horror washing over her, the girl declared it couldn't be anybody but *that horrible old hag, she could kill us, she'll never let me leave alive* and pulled him to run, run, run the way back.

What they didn't know, as we all do now, was that the villain of this story had in fact died days before. She hadn't anything to do with the horse—it is now assumed that the horse simply broke the rope on its own—and the hag's rotting corpse would be burnt with the tower in a putrid fire he would order within the week. But for that moment she was as big and fearful as the earth itself, and they charged through the forest as fast and desperately as any other fleeing victim.

Without the romance coloring a blackened forest into a gentle moonlit night, the dark now seemed to push on their fears and they staggered on even as their skins were streaked with weeping cuts, their clothes shredded by the catching limbs of the forest. Though they would make it, they panted to each other that much. *We're going to make it, my love.* As the palace crept up within their sights and the edge of the forest gave way to the river that divides the two worlds, they could almost believe so.

But this is a tragedy.

The poor girl, gasping from their flight and dizzy at the prospect of this glowing paradise before her becoming home, tripped in the unsteady ground and fell into the dark waters. He tried to help—by the Gods, he nearly drowned himself—but her hair at once took up the weight of the water and the braid may've well been a stone strapped around her head.

She sank to the bottom. They never could find her. And there she stays.

He vowed against loving then. It was frivolous. It wasn't real. The only thing that could follow opening one's chest to bare their heart is the sharpness of a blade when one's lover pushes a knife in, so he said. And so it was.

He did not wish to take a wife but he was, after all, a lord. And lords must have ladies. So he tolerates them—gives them a tight smile across the table, a brush on the mouth to pass for a kiss, a few weeks of solace at their early departures. But they know there is no love to be had, and that is what we all privately think these young things are driving themselves dead from, really.

Our lives were not built to have those kinds of fancies. We come into this world to work, to serve, to earn the occasional silver or thrill of a living child. What we get is all by our master's good graces, and we're taught from infancy not to expect very much.

The First Lady, speaking in the material, is not much more than some bones and a decayed braid settled in the deep of our waters. The First Lady, speaking in the unspeakable, is our mother. Our daughter. Our sister. The girl we just *pray* will be the one to find a life beyond our sights. Of happiness that's always swung, like her hair, above our stretching fingers.

There's a little place by the river, just past where we wash our thin skirts and draw water for our bare cottages. A flowering tree by the shore, a place of shade and rest on our odd hour off before the night snaps in the sky. What they take from our scalps we collect, hairs scooped up into pockets once they've left us alone. On this tree's branches hold the tied bundles of blonde, brunette, auburn, jet black, the rarity of red. Smooth or curled or coiled or kinked, knotted there by the tired hands of a visiting girl who just wishes, wishes.

MONROE AND MANSFIELD AT A PICNIC

S he'd been pushing 40 in a 25, flirting with a ticket she couldn't pay, but this was *it* baby: her big break, finally. And here she was going to blow it by being ten or god-damn-it-all even twenty minutes late. It was a possibility, a probability even, that she just would not surrender to, not for anything.

Rolling up close was her turn—a shortcut through a residential street she'd preplanned out. She pulled her car a hard left to make it. Had she not been racing to make an interview, to make her life back whole, she might've noticed how lovely, how springtime, the afternoon was thawing out to be.

The girl (though perhaps to say "the woman" would be more appropriate—she was 25 but built little, like she was still waiting on those last stages of puberty) dug her fresh-painted nails into the steering wheel as she weaved between the lefts and rights, just barely skirting around parked cars and the gray arcs of sprinklers. Seeing nobody around—no dog walkers on their regular loops or kids coming home from school or elderly men looking out at other lives from their porch—she risked bringing her speed back up again to 35.

Houses and cars and dead lawns blurred by. It was only until she drove past too many starter-model homes, until she had soared through too much unfamiliar suburbia, did she realize with that sinking *shit shit shit* feeling that she had taken the wrong turn somewhere. There was no room on the road to spin her car around and try to fix her mistake, no clear driveway to pull into and reverse out of. She was already 16 minutes late.

So okay. She'd try finding a cul-de-sac to loop through. She covered her car's analog clock with the restaurant's business card and kept going.

The only noise to be heard on that day, the only one really out there in this whole neighborhood built for life and people, was the air pulsing through her cracked windows and the rattle of an engine on its last trek. Of course the girl, in her bit-back misery, didn't hear any of this. She only heard the screams in her own head as she drove on.

The street seemed to widen up ahead, a sky peeking through the intertwined trees that framed the sidewalk. Moving on that one hope, that she could finally turn back the right way and somehow get the manager to believe that she would never be this late to any shifts and get a real apartment for herself and never have to look at that foul-fisted lover ever again, she put more weight on the accelerant and didn't even *see* the pole that came cutting into the front of her Buggy.

There was no time to brace for impact. She did not understand what was about to happen until after it happened. She never knew how her head had smashed through the windshield, how her seatbelt had tried so hard to hold her back that her collarbone broke. She did not see her body so unbelievably broken, her earthly remains tangled amongst the metal too badly to be taken out in one piece. She just knew she was dead—spare her the details, please.

The glass barely made a noise as it shattered and

fell onto the ground below, the asphalt covered in cutting sprinkles. The girl's car didn't beep or honk or give any indication that it knew what happened. It just stopped at its point of collision, never to run again. The card flew off the clock, which still blinked the time like a mocking finality of her life. She was 34 minutes late and she would never run again either.

The girl stayed calm, though. She didn't feel any pain or damage. She pulled her purse out from under the smashed passenger seat and stepped out of the car, minding the shards and pieces all around. Her heels clicked away from the scene and towards the park that the street had apparently ended into.

Up a hill in the distance, two blonde heads gleamed under the now full-out sunshine. The day had grown warm and breezy, springtime for sure. One of the blondes turned and saw her. She pulled an arm back and forth in a big wave.

"Hey!" the pleasant voice called out. "Come on up!"

The girl took the steps cut into the incline up to them. They were pretty women, movie star pretty, just a little older than the girl. They motioned for her to come sit on their blanket. She did. She was not uncomfortable.

"We've still got some wine and cherry pie." said the one with the longer hair, the one who had waved. "Please, help yourself."

The girl poured herself a glass of wine, cut herself a slice of pie. She took only one glance back down at her wrecked car, her last hope. On those worst nights her boyfriend always said, "You'll never make it without me." Sometimes she had believed it, sometimes she hadn't.

But the last time, the very last time as she was icing her eye and he called her dramatic on top of everything else, she thought he was full of shit. She'd finally thought he was full of shit, a living demon who would suck everything from her if she didn't get away already. That's when she saw the Hiring sign. She took it as a sign—you know, a *sign* sign.

Ha.

Eventually this really could be funny to her, that he was correct. She didn't last an hour without him after all. He was actually fucking right. But right now, now it made a big flaky bite of crust catch in her throat. She swallowed hard to push it down, this thing that felt like glue going down her stomach.

She had tried, hadn't she? She'd only been late in the first place because he wouldn't let her leave. She'd had to wait until he'd been tucked and drunk and asleep, and that took longer than she thought. Too long, as it turned out. And, well…here she was.

"Don't worry about that," the other woman said, a slight twinge in her smile. "It'll all get cleaned up soon."

The girl smiled back. She didn't want to spend her life waiting tables and cleaning motels anyway. There were too many problems she had been trying to fix. The women, all three, were just fine where they were.

She was just fine.

VIVISECTION

She didn't much care for frogs. They garnered only a little more compassion than insects. Still, she was glad to see the ones they were cutting in seventh-period biology were so hard and cold that they couldn't have possibly felt the scissors dig beneath their skin.

Phoebe was always her partner. Kay could at least count her blessings for that—out of all her senior classes without a single face that'd respond to even a "Hello" from a rumored dyke, she had Phoebe in this one. Sweet brown-haired girl she'd known all her life. Thank God for Phoebe.

Kay let her spread the thin limbs of their frog and pin its hands to the metal tray underneath it. Their little frog was dark and bumpy, still glistening a bit from the preservatives in the bucket from which it'd been pulled out by their teacher. Seeing was enough for Kay. Even with the gloves on, she didn't want to touch something dead. Phoebe was the one with the stomach for it.

Phoebe was the one who had experience with the dead, too. It didn't bother her any. She'd lived it: her dad died only a few years ago.

Kay recalled all too well the gray-blue pallor of Phoebe's father when he was stretched out stiff in the coffin, suited for final visitors. Really, it was the only thing she remembered from freshman year, this funeral. It would probably be the last thing she remembered before she was displayed for her own mourners, too.

Her mother had made her wear a pair of these

abominable *ladylike* black-lace gloves. Her protests went ignored over the argument that she had to *dress to respect*. That was the second-worst thing about the whole affair. She could still feel her hands sweat in that those goddam gloves as she clutched Phoebe throughout the service. When she finally pulled away, Kay left a perfect lace-dented handprint around her slender arm.

It was a sudden sort of death, cause inconclusive. Such a tragedy, people said. One minute a good man who may have had only a few transgressions—the next, on the floor with his wife shrieking over his body while the dog finished a sandwich that had fallen with him. It was speculated to be a heart attack, an embolism, something quick and invisible.

Phoebe was the perfect stoic. She thanked the many mourners as they lined up to give their sympathies, a small smile managed on her cherubic face. When the time came, she knelt at her father, raised her knotted hands up, and prayed. The scene of such a nice little girl in the act of mourning made even Kay herself feel shocking tears spring up like acid in her eyes.

It was when he descended into finality, dropped down into the dirt next to other big boxes containing his ancestors, that Kay felt her knees give out and she fell sideways into Phoebe. A gasp escaped from her lips as she collided into that small frame, a frame that was already bearing more than what even seemed possible. She already knew the earful she'd catch on the ride home, the lecture her mother would give about *not making such a scene, especially when people are talking enough and especially when the family is keeping a stiff upper lip, you theatrical girl.* But Kay couldn't hold it, not like Phoebe could.

"Don't cry," Phoebe had murmured into Kay's ear, the words sweet and special and just for her, only ever for her. "This isn't a sad thing. This is what we'd wanted, right?"

Phoebe didn't tell her, not explicitly. What she did say was all Kay needed to know to say yes. And she did say yes.

So Kay stood herself up. She wiped her eyes with those ugly gloves. She supposed Phoebe was right. She didn't deserve these tears, not with what they'd done.

She would let Phoebe handle the frog. Kay would do the writing and clean the tools. She slipped off the lab gloves. They weren't necessary this time. She rubbed her hands to get rid of the white, sterile powder the gloves left behind. This was a particularly sticky residue, the powder. Kay knew it'd take a couple hand washes to really get it off.

Cleanup comes later. For now, she settled into labeling their worksheet. Making sense of the entrails and organs were easy enough. Phoebe had pinned back the first layer of skin on the belly, nearly ready to work through the somewhat tough muscle next. Cut the frog, write the answers. These were tasks they could complete together.

Something neither of them could expect: movement. A sign of essentially impossible life. Kay was sure she must have been imagining the curling of its fingers and the quivering of its mouth, but Phoebe stopped her work just as she had. It could have been a folie a deux. Or it could have been the fucking frog wasn't dead.

Kay felt sick. The thing was wiggling in pain and she almost wished she could take her textbook and smash its head out of mercy. But Phoebe was staring at the belly, the limbs. She thought again and decided not to do anything, not right away. She'd let Phoebe think.

"Must be muscle reflexes," Phoebe said after maybe minutes of silence. Still calm, still the stoic. Nothing was ever a horror to Phoebe. "Post-mortem spasms."

"But maybe—"

"Oh Kay-Kay, it couldn't possibly still be *alive*."

Phoebe picked up the scissors and wiggled the two points through the layer of muscle. The frog seized up, one leg coiled so far into the air that the pin was almost knocked loose. Phoebe looked up at Kay. She knew perfectly well what was expected of her.

With one shaking finger, she pushed the pin back down and put the frog back in its rightful place. She sank her front teeth into her own lip to keep from making noise. She felt like the pin was going through her own hand.

"It doesn't hurt," Phoebe said, and Kay didn't know who she meant.

THE SEAMSTRESS AND HER SINNER

S he caught Pop's eye when she came walking out. He gave her the up-down, seeing the dress for what it was, then shook his head and smiled halfway. Try as Pop had to ensure Ana would never speak his language and thus regress to immigrancy, she still always understood him perfectly: *Yes, this is something you'd rather die than wear out in the world, I know. But please be nice.*

Ana had seen the light leaking under Mama's studio door on many of her 2 AM nightcap creepings to the kitchen and, yes, she was all too aware of how hard Mama had worked on this frilly thing. But, she'd never held her tongue when she felt like telling Ana that she ("personally, dearest") would much rather die horribly than be reduced to a divorcee like her.

As if Pop would ever break his sacred Catholic vows—he would always bear his wife as Christ did the cross. He did love her, though. And he loved Ana, loved her enough to take her back without a hint of shame. For Pop and Pop only, she bit down on her inner cheeks and passed on.

"How darling," Mama said appraisingly, her hands smoothing over the tiers in the skirt. "You look like a nice girl in this."

Be nice. Be nice. Be fucking nice. The words beat like the now-bleeding bite in her mouth. Ana could force herself only to nod and, when Mama motioned her to the mirror, to take the two steps forward and look up at the apparent nice girl Mama had made from discarded bolts of fabric left at the shop. She really did do a terrific job, especially with material that the real nice girls didn't want.

Ana had tried to be nice—for almost six years—and look where that got her. An embarrassing move home to Deerfield and her old bedroom back. She'd burned through most of her youth, and she had nothing to show for it. No, being nice did not a happy marriage make. It was the only lesson—and a hard-learned one at that—she got from her teens and twenties thus far.

She was not an educated girl. She could've been, she wanted to be. But apparently not enough. Ana told herself she never had the option to go to college. Truthfully, her parents probably could've worked something out and she definitely would've found a much better man like the rest of her old friends. She could've at least had a degree by now.

When they got married, she told herself she could be one of those little wives who take night classes while their husbands stay late at the bar. But then he didn't go to the bar. He only went to work and church —when he wasn't home, of course. Her husband was always home.

She figured then maybe she could have a little day job to fill the days while she waited to become a mother—he nixed that idea as soon as she said it. That…*man* thought she was better off staying at home, to be prepared for when they would have children. However, he overlooked the necessity of certain acts for conception to occur.

Not that she was a virgin. He couldn't at least leave her that much—once a month or so, he'd remember she was there and deign himself to the wonder of marriage. And he didn't have the decency to cheat or beat. At least then she would have a real *reason* for coming home, an answer people would understand and deem her nearly blameless

Some of those years were wasted waiting for him to blow things up enough to give her that excuse. It got to where she had to leave the room when her cousin started crying about her lush of a husband leaving for the neighbor's—not because Ana was so overcome with empathy, but because that black eye looked too beautiful to her. Her jealousy was sick and she knew it. But that didn't stop her from one day begging him to just hit her, hit her already, and let it be done.

Of course, he wouldn't. And it took him almost twenty-two seconds to even raise his gaze from the paper after that little outburst. Twenty-two seconds. She only waited—and counted—that long so she could look him in the eyes when she said it.

"I want a divorce."

As she was pulling things out of her drawers and throwing them into bags, cramming her stupid little clippings and cosmetics into the few empty spaces, she heard him reply from the dining table, where he did not bother to leave.

"Alright."

Alright. That did it—so went those six years with her supposed high school sweetheart. She was twenty-four and had, as Mama had so eloquently put it, reduced options when it came to a potential second husband.

Good old boys who worked with their hands all day and hopefully wouldn't put them on her at night. Widowers with children. An older man, maybe. Best case scenario was that Mama's friend's veteran son with a glass eye ("that you wouldn't even notice if I didn't point it out") who worked at the bank will accept the match and take her out of here.

And maybe it's because Ana had been so worn down by the years of apathy, the years of being likened to little more than the diploma hanging on his wall, that she actually agreed with Mama: this was the best she could do. She just had to hope he was nice enough and work his way up to maybe a manager and give her kids to go into a modest inland bungalow and afford at least one domestic vacation a year. That was her American Dream now.

He knocked softly, like the wood could suddenly give away. Pop went over slowly—his arthritis had been giving him more trouble lately—and answered the door. And Mama gave one last squeeze, one last command hissed into her ear.

Be nice. Be nice. Be nice.

Ana could try again.

TRIPTYCH OF THE INTERWORLD GIRLS

Irene O'Neil, County Mayo 1865

They call her Irene on paper, but there is a different word conjured on the tongue: changeling. Even the Hunger couldn't change that: a changeling. It's the true name their hearts hold—especially Mother.

The people of her village believe the real Irene was stolen by the Sidhe when she was not even a year old, and the Irene they know now is nothing more than some fae-made creature left behind in the crib as a poor substitute for the human babe that Mrs. O'Neil mourns to this day. And Mrs. O'Neil, she spends every one of Irene's birthdays keening down by the river. Today is Irene's sixteenth.

Irene is celebrating with nothing more than a nip of whiskey to numb another day working at lace for some sassenach's charitable wife. Irish lace made by rough Irish hands attached to a tired Irish body—none of which is worth very much in this world. It's almost irony that the only thing Irene has is the fear of everyone else, and sometimes that does pay out in scraps.

Women who won't so much as look her way at Mass come calling when Night pulls itself over the village, cloaking their pleas to the unbred girl in the anonymity and desperation that only the darkness can provide. Wayward husbands, lost sons, sickly children still half-starved—Irene has heard it all, and she's promised all sorts of folk fixes in exchange for old stews, broken baskets, and occasional bits of beef. It's one step above begging and one below whoredom, but sometimes it's all Irene has to keep her and Mother on this side of the veil.

They live, not well, but they live, and often only by Irene's nimble fingers and practiced words. Mr. O'Neil —for she cannot really call a man she never knew *Father*—was vanished before the real Irene was even born. Sometimes the British men and their British guns can make magic too, if only the blackest kind. And yet they are the ones who see them as the superstitious, the savage, the subrace that must be somehow saved. Yet, it is her own people who see her as something Other altogether.

It is said that Mrs. O'Neil had been diligent about keeping a pair of iron scissors under the crib to ward off the thieving fae. The real Irene was dangerously beautiful the way a jewel-heavy necklace is, and Mrs. O'Neil always kept a careful watch over the emerald of her eye.

But postpartum widowhood had worn her to the bone, worn her to the point where sleep once overcame her while still holding Irene by the hearth. This could have been just one in the thousands of cases of overlaying, but Mrs. O'Neil did not wake to a dead child in her arms; she woke up to a different one entirely.

This one was not the chatty girl who toddled about on ever-steadying legs. This one, she seemed not to know she was even there at all. Whatever was behind those eyes seemed stuck in another world, a world she would never quite leave. The village handywoman confirmed the terrible truth of this child, but it came with a small consolation: changelings hardly live more than a few months. Mrs. O'Neil was told to take it home and feed it what she could, and time would sort itself out.

The auld dear waited: days, weeks, months, years, until finally she had to accept that this thing would be the only child she'd ever have. And so it became Irene.

Irene is sixteen and still can't say whether or not she is truly a changeling. She's odd, yes, but inhuman? The question hangs over her head like a cruel god ready, waiting, to strike down with an answer and leave her dead either way. To be a changeling means being a creature after all, but then there is home awaiting her through the nearest fairy ring. But if she is the real Irene after all? The idea just can't be contemplated, at least not until she'd swallowed down enough drink to think without a stab of fear in her chest. She isn't drunk enough, but she tries to do it anyway.

She may have just been born a stranger after all. With her flaxen hair and sun-spotted skin she looks just like Mother, but everyone sees something somehow *wrong*. It doesn't take much: a too-hard blink, a restless hand, a sudden wince. They might not know how or what, but they know, and they always will. Wherever she goes—which, she is sure, will be indentured to America like most other useless girls—it will go with her. This curse, her only constant companion. They are all born sinners, but Irene was born punished. The thought trills down her throat and settles like ice in her stomach.

Irene checks for Mother before retrieving the little bottle of whiskey from under a loose floorboard near the door. She doesn't know when Mrs. Mallory will come calling with this offering again, but she finishes the last of it in one swallow anyhow. And it's gutrot, really, but it'll do. Already the terror of her own being has been anesthetized.

She puts her back to the wall and lets the liquor bring her down to the floor. Her blood feels heavy, but pleasantly so. It's a weight she wouldn't mind wearing around, if she can only figure out how to keep it from choking her like it has so many others.

But then she isn't like many others now, is she? Right now, it's funny, and Irene actually laughs. "Changeling," she whispers. She doesn't often say it aloud. It comes out halfway between a joke and a prayer.

"Changeling. Changeling. Irene O'Neil. Brutal Celt. Damned girl. Curious thing. Fae familiar. Poor child. But which is it, huh? Which is it?"

As always, an answer escapes into the air.

"Rachel Davis," Kentucky 1892

Nobody had minded until she started showing.

Mr. Davis brought her into his home as a servant girl when she was perhaps ten. Along with sewing and etiquette lessons, they gave her Jesus and their surname, though she would never be a part of the family. Taken from her own, yes, but not adopted into theirs. (That bitter thought brings a flash of her own mother, her ever-changing amber eyes, her bright voice that still haunts like a song in the night.) Rachel, as they called her, was more or less their charge who worked for her dinner.

They would never call her by her name, her real one. Any of *that talk* was not allowed out loud, and so she kept it all in. She's gotten good at that over the years.

At night she would keep her head awake and try to think: etsi, tsalagi, kalisete. Or was it kalisetsi? Too quickly did words begin to fall out of her ears like water in a broken pitcher. Eventually she could only keep her grasp on one, the name she was forbidden to say.

She last spoke it to an Indian census taker some-time during the previous fall in a halting tongue—Ta-ke-la-nowe. Neither she nor the white man knew how to spell it in English, so he had to write it down as best he could phonetically. Ta-ke-la-nowe. This is all she had left.

But that isn't quite true, at least in the material sense. As Rachel, she has a number of nice things: a pair of stiff shoes bought new, four overskirts, three still-white shirts, a leather-bound Bible, a pair of gold earrings, and a bed that is legally hers. She made him, Mr. Peck, put that in writing: no matter what, she got the bed. And there is even a decent chance that'd hold up in court.

Mr. Peck is her new benefactor. Mr. Davis had made the introduction, but it was her friend Mary who encouraged the actual arrangement. Mary was once 5/8th Choctaw, just enough that she needed a white guardian to decide what to do with the money her mostly-white Pa'd left her. Now, Mary is a state congressman's *kept woman* with her own apartments in Louisville. It's a decidedly easier life, no one could argue that.

She told Rachel that she ought to accept Mr. Peck's clumsy advancements and Rachel knew she was right. Mr. Peck is nice in that dullard's way, and she can only live in the Davis household for so long. It isn't love, of course, but it is a sort of freedom she will never find otherwise. There are many worse fates for a woman like her in this world.

When she is regarded about town, it was first only as a sort of curiosity. They (the foreigners, she likes to tell herself, the joke that's always funny) don't often see her people outside of Wild West shows. Her people were supposed to be gone by now, roped off in ever-shrinking reservations out in Oklahoma. And yet here she is.

By surprise or by shame, they look twice and then try not to look at her again. When they must speak with her in shops or on the street, they do so with careful politeness one would use with a stranger holding a rifle.

Everyone in town knows she is Mr. Peck's secret and everyone pretends not to. She is treated better than a freedwoman, if not like a lady of some other land (again, the joke). Mr. Shul lets her purchase anything on credit at the general goods store and Ms. Merriman serves her in the front room of the dress shop like any other white woman. Some call her just Rachel, but most say *Miss Davis*. Now, they're whispering other words toward her, words she'd care to not repeat.

It's strange, how her growing belly is both an abomination and an achievement. After all, is this not what all the schools and church missions are striving for? To plant the seed of civility and yield an American out of the Indian? They want them to disappear, to dissolve within white skin and disavow any life before they were United.

Well, this is exactly how it happens (one night a week after seeing whatever vaudeville act had come to town), but Rachel realizes now that they just don't like to be confronted with the fact in action. She mortifies them the way one of her *unsaved* sisters would probably mortify her, should she ever see them again. But she knows that reunion will never happen. Not now, anyway.

She never expected Mr. Peck to marry her, but now that is inevitable. He is a single man and, dullard he may be, honorable. It won't be like one of those fort marriages that made Rachel's mother, that made Rachel 3/4ths. He is a single They can do it under God and country—legally, Rachel is white. Eventually Rachel will be, she knows that.

Maybe not with this child (already she sees this son, whom she is sure is a son, marrying someone as externally Indian as him), but with the children afterwards. Will she one day be but a blight on their bloodline, or forgotten entirely?

Her world, which she didn't live in long to begin with, will die with her. She can't teach her children the things she barely remembers herself. Even etsi is not a safe thing to put in their mouths; one slip in front of the wrong people, and they may vanish to places people do not come back from. No, they will have to behave as *citizens* to be at all.

It doesn't feel like she is really losing anything. Home has been dead for a long, long time, long before she was even born. She was born to be like a ghost stuck between one world and the next; not allowed to leave where she's been, but never accepted back where she came from. She'd been taught such circumstances are only found in Purgatory, but she is not an unbaptized baby or some undetermined soul. She, Rachel, still walks the Earth, and there is not much she can do but patiently wait out this life. But she can give her child a chance.

She stands up, smoothes her skirts, and steps into the little courthouse. One paper, three signatures, and it will be done. Ta-ke-law-nowe will cease to exist forever. Only Rachel Peck can remain.

Still, she does remain.

Anne Irene Adsila Peck, Anywhere Now

Anne sits in her car toggling the Bluetooth connection on her phone on and off, on and off. Her AirPods are not showing up. Already that feeling is rising up in her throat. She tamps it down and tries again. On and off. On and off. On and fucking off. Nothing.

It doesn't take more than a couple seconds for her to understand that her AirPods are dead. When's the last time she had charged the case? She can't remember. Her fault, her fault.

It's coming up again. She gets a pair of earplugs from the glove box and shoves them in deep enough

to hurt. She's been spoiled by noise-canceling tech-
nology and she knows this won't be good enough, but
she has to pretend it will be. It's like what her mom
taught her as a kid: smile for long enough, and eventually you'll start feeling happy. She flips down her
driver mirror and practices. Her teeth show, but it's
disconcerting. She puts the mirror up. She breathes,
breathes again, and then grabs her tote and gets out of
the car.

She is half an hour early and there is a bar in the
plaza. Her hands instinctively itch for it: a cool dark
place out of the unletting sunny afternoon, an old
fashioned slid over the counter by a bartender who
doesn't try to make conversation. One drink would be
enough to turn down the lights and lower the volume
for the class, but not enough to risk a DUI after.

She's already at the entrance, one hand on the door.
She falters, starts to walk away, stops, walks back, and
then walks away again. But then she comes back a bit.
The bartender, an older Daytona-type woman, is
looking at her. Well, now she has to go in.

That excuse is good enough for Anne and she is
seated with a double she didn't explicitly ask for in
under two minutes. If the bartender noticed the large
yellow plugs stuffed in her ears, she didn't care
enough to ask. Bars are the one place Anne always
feels the distinct pleasure of being disregarded, of
being essentially alone in public.

The beadwork class inside the center starts at 5 PM.
It's about fourteen minutes away from her apartment
with traffic, so Anne left home at 4 PM. It is the first
time she has been out since a Sunday dinner with her

parents. Working from home allows her to go full hermit, but she has been trying to work on that.

There's no one else at the bar and while Lynyrd Skynyrd is playing, it's not overwhelming. Anne pulls out her book and reads. She tries to time herself: one swallow for every two pages. She checks the time on her phone with every page and cashes out before her drink is finished to be safe.

It bothers her immensely to only have a sliver of time to do something, especially when it is unplanned, but she's managing the best she can. Her AirPods were supposed to work. Alcohol, however, always does. One drink and then she can handle the overhead lights in a room with strangers.

But then it's 4:58 and Anne needs to pee and then she'll undoubtedly be late and the terror of walking in last and being seen like that means she won't be able to say so much as her name. Already she tries whispering to herself and it doesn't happen. It comes out like she's on drugs, and she's not even drunk. Yet.

What would she look like, walking in with whiskey on her breath when she knows just what alcohol has done to the community, one she barely has any right to be in? Sometimes she feels painfully stupid to even hear the word *reconnecting* in her head, too stupid to ever try putting it on the tongue. A blonde with a blood quantum. How all-American.

Thin ice already, Anne is. Thin ice easily broken now because she is (yes, fuck) a little tipsy and late and while it's supposed to be open to the public and Anne is (here she would explain exactly how, always so careful to show she is not the next pretendian)

Native she is not native to *right here* and she feels silly, always so very silly and the class was free to register for, anyways.

The bartender—Terri, she overhead the only other patron call her—is only a little annoyed when she asks to open another tab. She can always learn the basics on YouTube.

She is disappointed in herself, but not as much as she thinks she should be. This isn't what Anne should be doing and while she is so unavoidably aware, she doesn't quite believe she can figure out how to do something else. The only way she can go out in the world is if it's in these small, dark corners of it. Everywhere else is just too much.

Maybe one day she'll save up enough to get a little cottage in the Irish countryside or buy back land in Georgia and be done with it, but for now this is how she knows to live. Tomorrow she will try to try differently. But as for today? She will need to Uber home.

And she will sign up for the class next month.

CONSORT, 1953-1958

Miss Lucy was nice enough. Compared to the other ladies I cleaned for, she was the nicest. Paid me just like an adult. The others would try to barter—said I didn't need as much since I was only a schoolgirl, never mind the excess they shed on their own daughters. She treated me like the age I ought to have been in every which way.

Miss Lucy lived alone and rarely had more than some trash and dishes that she just couldn't bother with. And she never made me tackle anything really gross—no sludgy sinks or sex-stained sheets like the rest. Miss Lucy could even be cool. She was the first person to tell me that "it's like getting ketchup outta the bottle" joke and offered me her high-end-hand-me-downs (or, as my neighbor said about the labeled shirt I prided in on weekends, it was a *hand-me-the-fuck-ups*). But still—

I hated doing the Altar Room. It was the easiest one to take care of, granted, but it never failed to give me the horror-movie-heebie-jeebies. And, yeah, it would've been a cool setup in somewhere like the House of Blues or the Hard Rock, but those shrines in a pretty young (maybe 30?) woman's home screamed of something being just fucking *off*.

Friday afternoons were for the Altar Room. Miss Lucy showed me the first time how careful she wanted it—moving through the room like a bomb might blow at the slightest misstep—but she was rarely there afterwards. That was the other thing I liked about her: she sensed that I like being alone, and left me to it.

I'd let myself in at the very end of each Friday

cleaning and spend the next two hours wiping the light layers of dust and red wax that had settled on the mantels and trading out the candles for a new pack that she'd always have ready in the garage. She probably went through something like sixty of them a month. I think Miss Lucy would keep the candles burning through all the days and nights, but I wouldn't know for sure. I wasn't in there otherwise.

Thankfully, I didn't have to light them or anything. She insisted that there was no need for me to refill the little offerings of whiskey or do any real active participation. But, I mean, sometimes I'd take a hard look at the gold-on-suede portraits of Johnson, Jimi, Elvis, Morrison, Keith, Sid, Kurt, Cornell and wonder if there really was something to them. Maybe, like Luce'd say later, I was itching all along. I don't know so much about that.

I would have liked to think I knew my rockstars, but there was another portrait that I just couldn't place. Head-to-toe portrait on the back wall of an unidentifiable man. Not unnoticeable, though—he fit that whole tall, dark, and handsome thing. Light eyes, the kind that pop up against features like that. Sometimes I'd stare especially at him and try to place that face, those eyes, that half-smirk etched on there, but I never could. I was too afraid to ask Miss Lucy. So a mystery it remained.

Of course, there had to come that Friday afternoon when I had finished my work and was just looking at the good-looking stranger when I heard Miss Lucy come up behind me and ask:

"You wanna know?"

I turned around. I didn't nod or say I did or anything, but I stood there. No turning back (we joke now that it's like I knew it was going to be my own sort of Good Friday). She was smiling.

"Carmen, sweetheart, let's go sit down," was all she said, and I followed.

That's my name, just so you know. That's me—I'm Carmen. Even with everything else, that hasn't changed.

We eventually get to That Chat on the plushy chairs in the living room. Lucy knew that the whole thing would be too much for me if I was surrounded by them, you know, in that windowless room. We had the LA sun warming the carpet under our feet as she talked, and as things got more and more, I'd dig my toes into the grounding heat and feel alright with everything.

Not that anything was really overwhelming. That it wasn't too much to take, that's what I really don't get. Why I didn't just claim I had another job to get to and not show up the next week or ever again. Why I just sat in quiet fascination as she started by making sure I understood that

"I showed up dressed like the preacher's girl: bobby socks, underskirt, that whole thing. The boy I came with, the poor kid kept eyeing all the girls in their little swimsuits and he was stuck with *me*. Lakeside concert in the thick of July, and I refused to show anything more than my forearms. Well.

It was wild for me, to be sneaking out with a boy. Gone to hear the 'devil's bop,' as Daddy had denounced it. But then he'd been dead nearly a year, and Mama was too caught up with her new husband and baby to pay me much mind. I still reckon she'd have just about died too, if she ever knew that her goody-Godly girl had taken a ride from an older boy to see some guitar band.

They weren't famous—never would be—but that didn't matter. I was there to try something wild, and this seemed fitting. The dead preacher's only child, and here she was wanting to get some sort of stir. And you smart enough to figure I got it, huh?"

"I would have to imagine, yes."

She smiled like I actually said something clever.

"Sure as shit. When he came out, when he threw out those first couple words—oh! I'll tell you, I still get the fucking chills."

She actually shivered then, her eyes glazed a little with the still-in-love look. And her nipples became ever-so-there through the thin fabric of her tank top. At the tender age of 18.5, I'd had yet to feel something like that.

"They called him the No-Name Man. I call him… well, other things now, but he was just the No-Name Man that night. And *man*, he had these eyes that'd lock up and right through you, like he could see right through your clothes and everything else. They were blue-grey then and mean sometimes, but then sometimes almost innocent like a child's.

And yeah, course those eyes had to happen on me. That did it. Just that. I stood at the very back of the crowd, all the way to the shore, stuck all moony for him through the rest of his set.

At the last clap, he came to me. Walking, floating

kinda, through all these bare babes calling to him, and he came to me. And he said, 'You're the girl,' and of course I just had to nod along with him. I was whatever he said, that's how I felt about that.

He took my hand and pulled me past the girls chanting like confused sirens, past the passed-over boys flicking ash on the sand, past even my poor date bugging at me like he was watching a car wreck. I remember blowing a little pity-kiss at him. He was a nice boy, but he wasn't no No-Name…Carmen?"

"Mmm?" I felt like a lizard on a heat rock in that living room. If I had closed my eyes any longer than a blink, I would have fallen asleep immediately.

"It all moved so dreamy-like. He was pulling me into this cabin on the lake with a bonfire out back and the real owner freshly dead in the shed and nobody else around, and yet I kept enough of a head on me to awaken that morning still unsplit and sealed.

You understand, sealed? Not *whole*, because whole means you get broken later. Not that I didn't want him to break me, in that vulgar sort. But I know you've felt how delicious it is to pull back, even for only a little while. You get me."

She wasn't wrong. I'd been putting off the boy who took me to the movies going on five weekends in a row. It always went the same: he'd pick me up during daylight and say hello to Mother and buy me my own popcorn box and then put his lips on me when we pulled back into my driveway after. It'd somehow always work out that an Iggy Pop song would play when he did it.

I'd let his hands stray only as far as the hem of my

t-shirt before slipping out the passenger side with one more closed-mouth kiss and my prettiest Virtue of Diana's smile. I wasn't really waiting, though. I just didn't feel like it (or, at least, not with him).

Of course, after everything, I don't wait on anything anymore.

"Between beers and French kisses and fumbling around in the dark, he murmured a whole new life into my ear. It'd be Heaven, sorta. A forever state of parties, pools, drinks, drugs, music.

God, the music! I would've done it all for just that. It might seem so easy to say that in this nice house and everything, but I do mean it. And anyway, I had to go through Hell to get it."

Of course she did. Of course nothing in this loose life could come free. I'd learn it well myself.

"There's always one condition to go with him. 'The ride's toll,' that's what all the girls've called it. And the ride doesn't last—this here does, this goes on for fucking ever—but what you give up is worth it, worth so much more than what it did before.

I still got all my fingers and toes—look, see?—but what he wanted felt like a whole arm, some physical piece of me. He'd come out and said it by sunrise. For him, I had to prove all earthly allegiance and sacrifice anything that could keep me from him.

That's the way he put it, 'all earthly allegiance.' His type of evil comes in eloquence, honey, and it always sounds like poetry coming out of his mouth. But what would you think he'd ask from me, with talk like that?"

"Kill your family."

It just tumbled out. God. Oh my God. I had heard too many stories like this before: boy hooks girl, girl enchanted by boy, but then dear old dad gets in the way. It always ends the same. I waited for the shock of confirmation, for having to hear how she did it, but she only smiled.

"Nah." She laughed. "As far as I know, Mama got cancer in the seventies and it's not nice to say, but my little sister has always been a little slow to get married or have any babies. When she goes, it'll be just me. But neither of them ever knew that I was, still.

But I know exactly where they are. Mama got put in one of those above-ground tombs; I pay for sissy to stay in a good facility in Fort Lauderdale. And Daddy —well, of course I'll always have to know where Daddy is.

My No-Name had said I gotta give up what's got me back. He told it like a diagnosis, like Daddy had been but a tumor or parasite. I had to ex-cise him, that's what he'd gotten around to saying. No-Name could smell his meanness still clinging to my skin. I couldn't keep being the preacher's girl if I was gonna be his.

And so I told him Daddy was dead. And he told me knew. But he said so long as his bones still remained a-rattlin' on this earth, I would never be free of my old man and I could never belong to the No-Name Man. So I put two and two together—I was a smart girl, really, and I understood what he meant. Do you get it, darling?"

"Well," I had to admit, "not really."

She smiled and shook her head a little, like it was a

naughty joke she had to explain to someone much younger.

"No-Name meant for me to go out to Daddy—you know, to where he was buried—and dig him up. So I did that, although I'm making it sound like nothing. Getting him up took more time and tears than it did to drop him down there! I spent the entire next night digging and digging and digging. Must've been a real sight—I was sobbing with every shovelful.

But I was gonna do it. Didn't matter how hard it was or how much it hurt to do it. I'd found something I loved more than life itself, especially more than what was left of Daddy. And we gotta do what we gotta do and alla that.

I couldn't actually lift his casket out of the ground, when I finally hit on it. I had to crack it open right there in the hole. And there he was—nothing more than a set of mossy bones in his best Sunday suit. Didn't even smell, if you can believe that. Just kinda like the damp scent of a worn-out book.

I wasn't scared or sad or nothing. I felt like I was looking at one of the chickens Mama'd kill, like something that needed to be processed. I used the shovel to break his skeleton up into pieces and threw them one-by-one out of the hole. Then I just threw it all into a bag and left. Wasn't too heavy, either. I didn't bother covering his grave—nothing was gonna matter pretty soon, so best not waste myself on anything I didn't need to do.

No-Name'd told me of a spot about a mile into the woods. He'd been real clear about that part: start at Marker 42, walk straight, and eventually you'd hit it.

The sky was starting to warn of dawn when I came upon the clearing. I dumped the bag in the middle of the clearing and dragged some good sticks around it before setting the whole thing ablaze.

I didn't know the first thing about forest safety or any of that—I could've easily burnt the place down, me with it. But, you know, I had someone looking out for me. He made it all pretty simple.

Bones don't burn as easy as you'd think, though. I had to finish the job by grinding them down with rocks like some primitive. All said and done, the ash came out to no more than a cup or two. Imagine—all that, for a few handfuls of sandy ash! Amazing what we can be brought down to.

He'd left a cup out there for me. Nothing special, just this little glass. I scooped what I could into the cup and took it to the nearby river. You think you know the rest from here?"

"Honestly?" I said slowly, trying not to notice the shadows shifting around us. "I couldn't tell you."

"Guess I'll have to." But she didn't say it meanly. I later learned that this is what sealed my deal. "I just took a little water to mix with the ashes, and then I drank 'em.

That's right, No-Name had me drink my own daddy down and piss him out. Judgment Day ever come, Daddy's not gonna be able to rise. His soul isn't even around—this kind of thing wipes even the spiritual remnants of a person. I rid myself of every last trace of him, from this world and the next and then the one after that.

Daddy doesn't exist except within my memories

now. Even then, he's fading from me. He's fading all the time. There are different kinds of deaths you can fall to, and Daddy died in a way few ever have. And I killed him—completely and forever.

Every girl's got a different task. Whatever's the hardest and cruelest thing she can do, he has her do it. And when it's done, she can never turn back. Ride's toll is always one-way. That morning, I achieved earthly immortality and got my run with No-Name. And it's worth it—oh Carmen, I promise you it's worth it. You see that, don't you?"

I nodded. Even if I couldn't quite understand how, I knew that it was. She was offering me a new life, a life that was actually worth living and which lasted for forever. It wasn't like being turned into a vampire or some ghoul in the horror stories. It was warm and light and beautiful. I felt dizzy, drugged even. Yes, yes, yes, I wanted this. I wanted it.

"Carmen, darling," Luce said, "why don't you come into the Altar Room with me?"

I followed her back down the hallway and into that room. It wasn't creepy anymore—I got it now. She gently grabbed my shoulders and guided me toward his wall. I wasn't nervous. I waited, patiently, as she whispered in my ear.

"You'll have to be on your own now." She gave me one squeeze of reassurance before she backed off, closing the door behind her. I was ready.

And as his figure started to take shape and come out of the portrait, I was not afraid. It was simply my turn.

FINDING SIREN

There were a lot of things to be avoided around Pale Dale's open front window following June 6th, 1961. Dark church clothes, backyard bells that chimed a harmony when the wind picked up, mucky flowers kids took home from the swamps, any word that could ring too close to *her dear name*, and, most severely, water.

It was almost three days after that he could finally take a little bourbon through a straw after Father John convinced him that he *needn't die just yet*. A distasteful yet popular joke was that Pale Dale *mighta saved a coin without the wife, but he's saving stacks without the showers!*

Even if it was true, few could have confirmed it. As soon as a ceremonial casket was lowered into the scraped ground of her family plot, Pale Dale turned around, walked the four blocks home, shut his door, and never opened it again.

Maybe if he had family around, things could have been different. Maybe. But he only had a mother back in Naples. Pale Dale was one of the only people who weren't born-and-bred, and they hadn't had enough time to make their own family. There was nobody, save the priest, who dared breach his home to help him.

The four-count households surrounding his little one-bedroom felt so sorry and so afraid of his famous grief that they went as far as to cut their sprinklers, and the once proudly-lush lawns rapidly dried and died in that merciless Florida fever. The pale brown ghosts of grass first marked only the few closest neighbors, but it soon grew into an en vogue display of condolence.

It was only a few weeks before a green yard was considered impolite, even gaudy. Any passing travelers (because nobody but locals got outta their car in Pantano) might've looked out their window and exclaimed something like *they must have some kind of disease around here!* and they weren't really wrong.

A sister of the neighbor of his mother in Naples reported back that their last phone call wasn't much more than Pale Dale swearing and swearing that he'd *find her even if just a little piece Mama really* and if his mother weren't so ill-gotten by gout, she would have made a drive down to bring the maddening man home.

This new piece of gossip for the Main Street whisperers returned a few weak suggestions of *checking in with a casserole perhaps,* but the consensus was that yes, by God, he oughta leave. His patio overlooked the very scene of the one tragedy to have occurred in Pantano (of course, a few of their boys would get shipped to the wars and never come back, but those were a sort of safe death, far removed from the still-living, not the horror that occurred within a mere mile radius), and certainly no grief can be lifted if he was left to sit and fester in it like that. But the other part of it, the collectively unspoken part, was the relief it'd bring to everyone else.

To be rid of the gray, thinning face that occasionally blinked out that front window—well, that would be a selfish prayer answered. And so the town pushed their sorry clucks in his direction and then mutely prayed, prayed, prayed for him to be gone.

And then, after, they prayed for forgiveness.

Passed through the many mouths of the town were two different narratives concerning what a group of hunters happened upon on the heat-swollen afternoon of August 12th, 1961. The first is romantic, glamorous even, a fitting and sweet enough of an end to etch onto a wooden plaque put on the spot sometime later (a curious attraction that draws a summertime pilgrimage even today).

The lore goes something like this: some days before the 12th of August in 1961, the widower that was once Pale Dale paced the worn track of his once cozy little home. The house had fallen into a bit of a state already; it sagged as though it had been suddenly emptied out, yet the faded walls seemed to tighten without their lady by each colorless sunrise. From outside it looked like it was liable to collapse in on itself any day now.

Pale Dale paced. And he smoked. He took to keeping all his windows open in those last weeks, and the exhales of an endless cigarette in his hand trickled out into the almost-night air. It was sunset, people suspected. There's no source for this, but people started saying it: the last violent flames of the sunset had lit the walls in gold, threw the shadows long and slanted. This is what it looked like on that day. When it happened.

What happened on this day, whenever it had been, was something crept in and finally reached him. Not a person. Certainly not the community. It was the full-bodied voice that once led the choir and lured Pale Dale down to the nothing of Pantano. He froze at the first catch of that well-loved lilt, his body lurching slightly forward at his sudden stop. His Marlboro slipped between slackened fingers and hit the side of his bare foot.

If he felt it, he didn't give it any notice. A little burn mattered not. The impossible possibilities hung like humidity as he listened to her sing another verse in the wild that stretched only a few hundred feet from the home that seemed then to be squeezing, squeezing him to nothing if he didn't get out already.

The action that he sprung into was quick and final. He left through the backdoor he didn't bother to shut (they'd later find all sorts of wild things that took up residence in the house) and closed the gap between them within four choked breaths.

And people like to say she was waiting for him there, her hair hanging in loose curls against her face, dressed in a gentle white cotton, a true Lily of the swamp. He fell to his knees before her. She smiled and stretched out her arms.

It took several rough churns through the Pantano gossip mill to work the fable into something smooth and palatable enough to present even to his mother, a worn-out woman debilitated by gout and grief, at that second service of the summer. Contrary to every small town's penchant towards the unpleasantries, the foul of the truth was rarely spoken of.

Some knew. Some guessed it. Some saw that gap and filled it with stories too spectacular to be believed by anyone. Some had enough sense to see that the real story was somewhere in the center of all the talk. And the smart ones, the smart ones knew to leave it well enough alone. There were things in this world that were better not shared.

The hunting party who stumbled into the scene— those men who saw the baked body lying in the marshy grass, who discovered the pearly bone clutched in its withered hand—had the decency to not pass on the details. The rest of the town, ignorant of what they'd been spared from and starved of everything except for the vaguest idea of what really happened, talked and talked and talked until the tragedy turned into only a tired legend.

A restless little man in the 80s decided it'd make for a hit play at the community theater. There were a few cries raised for *moving on from all that*, but he pushed and pushed until it grew to a moderately successful run and a blurb in the paper. Their Pale Dale was a boy from the pepper plant with a slight limp and an endearingly shy smile; that She was a hometown-beautiful high school girl who had no lines.

After an almost-full closing night, almost everyone could nod their heads and agree *it was a nice little play after all* and then let it drop from their minds entirely. It felt like the closest to catharsis the town could get. And they could only tell the same story so many times.

But the little man thought he had something big. Big enough to try taking it to the cameras in Hollywood. Not the one only an hour away, as his family had hoped he meant; the place that seemed, to the people of Pantano, to be at the very end of the world itself. So he packed his beat-up Ford and set out one morning with that kind of mythic ambition that had some people even believing that *he just might be the kind of small-town boy that makes it there!*

But, of course, those high hopes were leveled when he quietly pulled back into his parents' darkened driveway a few months later. Some tried prodding him about his time there, but they couldn't get him to give them much more than a shrug.

And really, they didn't need much more than that. It was a thing too bitter to tell by the tongue: Pantano had itself a precious little tale, a star-crossed thing that rivaled the likes of those kids in Verona and the couple who tried getting out of the Underworld. But the Pantano Lovers were even better, because they were a true two—they lived and loved and died and left behind bones on their own land, not just one paper.

Everybody could claim their own little stories with the couple because they really had existed, right there, not all that long ago. And that *real as our own* blood they spilled had watered a history that grew into what they had under their most current sun. Even the ones who mostly dismissed *the old incident* would give it that much.

But it wasn't something to be taken further than their own little town. That was where the little man had made his mistake, trying to bring what was so distinctly *theirs* and make it stretch past its true reaches. And that was where the people learned that their story was safe, so long as it was kept inside.

And so it's been, and so it'll probably always stay,

at least until the town is finally wiped out by resort construction and golf courses and everything is forgotten like it was never even there. Because outside of Pantano?

Nobody gives a damn.

THOUGHTS FROM ONE OF THOSE
GIRL-TYPES THAT DISAPPEAR.

I know exactly how you could kidnap me.

I work at a grocery store—old place lit like a grave, semidead customers shuffling over linoleum and dust. My feet always hurt and my hands stay dirty no matter how much soap or scrubbing I commit. But that's all I'll say about the misery. My woes of minimum wage, I've learned, find no sympathy from anyone aside from myself.

Carts, sun, perpetual collection. Walk an old woman out like you're supposed to and get rewarded with endless laps around the lot looking for corporate property. But though my feet stay on its track (no matter how much they wanna just walk right off, right around the corner and never come back again), I let my mind wander whichever way it likes.

And I've been thinking.

There are a couple things you can get away with here. Somewhere along my time bagging—between the *triple bagged in paper for the wine please don't mind all the wine* and *oh no I forgot my totes oh here they are why don't you just go ahead and take my stuff out of the plastic and repack everything and I'll wait outside for you*—I always have the same contemplation of robbing a cashier.

I don't mean anything personal; I mean robbing the company stuff, that is. The Man, the abuser. I would never think to take 80-year-old Darlene's purse when she goes on break, oh no no *no*! No, I think of the cash in the drawer one could so easily take and be gone before anyone caught a clue.

And it'd be *so* easy. All you'd need to do is tell

them to give you the money. That's it. We've been told to obey, even if there isn't a weapon. You just never know and the company sure doesn't want that liability. They make too much money to really care about a couple hundred, anyway.

You could come in my lane with a small item that'd need one of the paper bags. Come early in the morning, right at opening. Slip the cashier a note, typed, and remind her to stay quiet. It'd look just like she was giving you cash back.

You'd wear a disguise. Nothing crazy—simple, insignificant. Something to let you blend back into the static as you'd walk away. Preferably, walking away with me.

Because in my head, I'd be bagging it. That's the most important thing, that's what excites me, the bagging. Helping you rob the store, helping you out to your car like I've been trained. Maybe I'd come back in a little while afterwards, tears slipping down my ruddy cheeks as I shook *Sir, Sir, there wasn't anything more I could do*. Or, maybe, I'd be your captive across state lines, a figure in the backseat as the sirens wail behind you.

I think about that the most. You couldn't rob the store if you wanted to get away with me—the police would be too quick on your trail. But really, it'd be easier to steal me, their dedicated little first-job girl, than their money.

Come at night. The store usually gets hit with a wave of soccer moms grabbing quick chicken dinners right before close, but the parking lot stays almost entirely empty. Come in on a scooter. We have to go out after the scooters; nobody would bat an eye.

Come in my lane. Get everything you'd need: trash bags, the little coiled ropes by the front, bleach, a knife. Make me watch you purchase it, make me bag up my own fate. Give me that first thrill of fear as you smile and the cashier can't think of anything other than her own dinner.

Park out at the furthest spot in the back corner. Our cameras only extend to the third row. The lot is so still in the dark, so quiet, so very *private*. Most nights it's just me and the lonely rattle of cage on pavement for hours on end. Because nobody wants to be out in this area without the sunlight and public to protect them. They fear the dark, the bogeyman snatcher. They fear exactly this. But I'm right behind you, wheeling down farther and farther than I'd ever wish to follow.

Don't make it obvious with a van. I'd expect something a little more discrete from you, something a little smarter than that. I know how you ought to best toy with me, trust you can do it right.

You'd tell me to set your things in the trunk. And you'd tell me to put them far back, that witch in the oven trick. And as I reach deeper and deeper into the back seat, you'd rise up from that scooter and loom, phantom shadow, right behind me.

(I'll keep what happens next strictly in my imagination, a beastly little detail I'll turn over later when it's dark and quiet and just me again.)

Why would you want me? I'm not the most beautiful thing to set upon, but I am young. I know how it is we must wreck through you, yeah? New-minted women are a fickle thing. Winking at the construction man as we pass on the street, horrified at the thought he'd peep in through the window later.

And maybe I am. Maybe I know what I wore that red lip for. Maybe I know how a schoolgirl in ballet flats dancing past you on the sidewalk makes you lose control. Maybe I'm trying to bait the monster. Maybe I really am as wholly twisted as you are. But I'll never digress. That kind of confession I'll always smile to myself as your torture, a little withholding against your zip-ties and pacing about the motel room.

Kill me, keep me, whatever. I'll never know much of a difference. Perhaps one tired night you'd be too loose with me, slip a little and forget to check how tight I'm tied to the bed. I'd finally break that one rope around my wrist I'd been working on all week and kill you. Stab you, screaming for help, while you sleep.

I'd come back out into the world covered in your blood and ready for my *20/20* tell-all. It wouldn't be just a legal murder, love—I'd be a goddamn hero. Memoirs and meeting with celebrities and not even one more shift in Hell.

But I could never really know how it'd end. Maybe I die by your hand, or by some horrible accident; or you die by my hand, or by the beautiful chair waiting at Raiford. Or maybe we sit there in wherever, holding each other captive until the end of time. Either way, in any way, I'm sure it'd be a real nightmare.

I close tomorrow night.

SKEEZY GEEZER

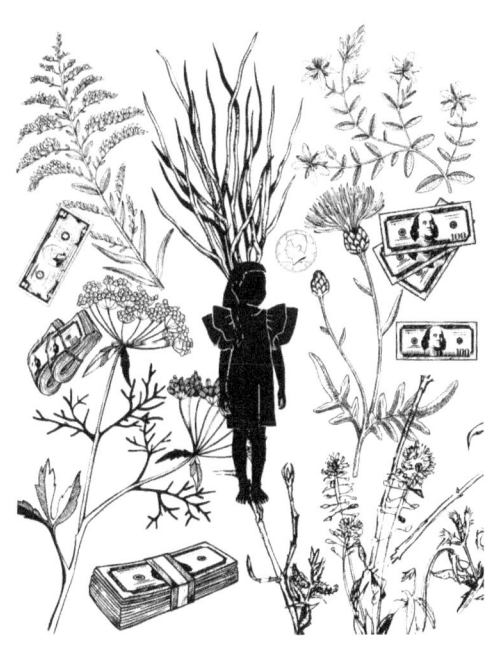

L ala made five dollars a week pulling the weeds in Mr. Fred's yard. She started out at only three dollars, but he decided she deserved a raise once she made it to middle school since *a girl needs her mall money*. That brought it up to five.

With respect to what a sixth grader could get, though, it was a good job. There was never any set time or standard she had to make; usually she'd just stop along her walk home from the bus stop and pluck any stray growth that'd popped up overnight.

There were two types of weeds that she had to look for, and there were two different things that she did with them: flowers for her room and true weeds for the trash. She took the frizzy little wildflowers home to sit in a shallow vase on her dresser. The thin, V-shaped stalks got chucked into the carport garbage bin. Couldn't do anything else with them, unfortunately.

Those were known as Bahia Grass, native to Central Florida but unwanted on the lawns. Lala'd looked it up. Named too nice for itself, she thought. Bahia grass. Sounded almost like *Bahamian* to her. It bothered her: a plant that grew here naturally, named like it came from somewhere else, deemed unsightly by the people who moved in and made lawns in the first place. It felt uncomfortably familiar for Lala, who was a bit of a weed herself.

All the Bahia Grass piled up in the bin made her feel bad. Useless deaths of lesser life forms, decaying without so much as an audience. She'd tried decorating her room with them like the wildflowers, but it just looked dirty. In less than a weekend Ma said they gave off *a really green stink La*, threw them out in the kitchen trash, and lit one of her soy candles.

Ma was probably the one who got her the little job with Mr. Fred. Lala barely even knew the neighbors in the condo above, but Ma was one to chat up everybody. In between swing shifts, Ma liked to knead at her server-swollen feet and complain that Lala was *much too quiet*.

She wasn't wrong. For all the trouble Ma'd went to for her, she didn't for much of a conversation partner. Lala just never *had that much to say*. And Ma could only take a listener so long.

So Ma would go out: with coworkers, to White Wine Wednesday at the other Francesco's, for even just a walk down the street. Lala figured Ma had went down that part of the street—Rex the pit bull pulling her along—and called out a hello at the old man who sat out in the driveway. She couldn't care enough to ever know for sure, though.

There weren't many rules from Ma, as far as it went about the weeding thing. Ma knew she was *u smart enough girl* and Lala knew to pull to the root. She didn't have to worry about his St. Augustine grass. He had sprinklers to keep it from browning, mostly, and Reggie would mow it on Saturdays.

Reggie was Lala's *deadbeat's* sister's kid down the other end of the street. Lala knew the right word was "cousin," but she also knew not to use it unless she wanted to poke a fresh rant out of Ma. He was a boy, and fourteen, so he got to make ten dollars a week doing that. He'd try to rub it in when he came around.

But Lala didn't mind. Lala knew that when she was fourteen, she could make ten dollars *an hour* babysitting. Reggie couldn't, because he was a boy. And Lala could, kind of, rub that one in.

She got paid on Friday afternoons. Mr. Fred would watch her from his plastic chair as she'd check over the yard. He'd sweat in the heat; she would not.

"It look good?" he'd ask when she'd walk up his way.

"Yu-huh."

"You sure?" But he meant it like a joke.

And Lala would nod, and she'd shift her feet. She didn't like to look at him. She was still at the age where she could take the old or ugly only in little glances. He had thick white hair clustered up his nostrils and growing in a triangle on his chest, but only a couple strands still on his head. His scalp was probably the darkest skin on his body. Sunscreen would've helped, Lala always thought. A hat, at least.

Mr. Fred never wore a hat, or shoes, and usually no shirt either. He would sit there rubbing his white triangle while teasing Lala while she waited to just get her money and go. He'd be waiting for a smile or a little fake laugh, usually. Usually, Lala would end up giving that to him. And then he'd give her the money, and she'd go, and she'd have another week until it was time to come back and play the whole thing out again.

It always went so same-same that Lala could've called it a "ritual" or like Mama's server routine that brought home all the fives and tens and sometimes twenties that she'd have to help sort out for the weekly bank deposit and that Mama didn't know if *it really beats a sit-on-my-ass job*. Especially in a land without seasons, they lived a life so repetitive that neither could tell each week from the last. Lala didn't mind it, though. Repetition made magic, and magic made money.

The ritual, or routine, or whatever, with Mr. Fred was only ever different when he didn't feel like getting up from his chair to put Reggie's payday in his mailbox. On those couple times, he just trusted her with that money *to give to who earned it*. Lala had to, obviously, because they'd all know otherwise.

One time went different though—like actually different. It was one of the last Fridays of sixth grade, and Lala could say that for sure because she was out at 1 PM instead of 3 and didn't have her backpack. It was also the Friday that it first occurred to Lala that maybe Mr. Fred didn't actually live in that lawn chair, because it was empty when she came down his street. She blinked at that revelation, at the idea of Mr. Fred being anywhere but there, until she figured that then he must be inside. She decided to go up and knock on his door.

He was home. He made a noise when she knocked, and then it was a minute until he actually opened the door.

"You early," he said with something like an accusation.

"It was a half-day," she said. She straightened up for some reason. "We only had two classes."

He sucked in his cheeks at that and looked at her. She looked at her dirty flip-flops, at his bare feet.

"They took a cut outta all my paychecks to give you only two classes?" He was laughing, kinda, but it didn't seem like something that Lala was supposed to laugh at with him. She stood there. "Well, you might as well come in."

"I'm alright—"

"It's hot."

It was. Even the backs of her knees were starting to get damp. And she could feel the blast of his AC from the entrance. It wasn't some great hesitation. She went in.

His living room was cool and dark. Lala could've napped in there, if it'd been quiet. If he hadn't been there. The news channel that Ma hated was on. Mr. Fred waved a hand at the couch like saying "sit," and Lala sat.

"I'll get your money," he said.

He walked behind her into another room. She could hear a drawer opening, some swearing, and then his steps on the tile when he came back out. He gave a low grunt as he lowered himself down onto the seat next to her.

He had a bill in each hand: a twenty in his left and a five in his right. He held them up to make sure Lala saw.

"You know that one is worth more than the other, right?" Lala nodded. He nodded with her. "Good, I'd figure. How much more is this over that?"

"Fifteen."

She was twelve, not two. To him, she thought, maybe it was all the same. Like how she figured he was either a hundred or sixty and it didn't make any difference to her what he was really. Young is young and stupid, and old is old and stupid. All the same. "Twenty is four times the five."

"Guess you only need those two classes, then," he said. He could've been trying to compliment her. "I'm betting you want this twenty instead of the five?"

"Yes."

But she just couldn't see him trusting her to learn how to use the lawnmower, and that was more than what Reggie was making anyhow. And she didn't really want to do more than what she was doing now. Still, more money was always worth it. She was old enough to know that much.

"I got an easy thing for you then," he said. "Something so easy you can do it right now."

She knew exactly where this was going. She started weighing out whether it'd be worth the headache to help him fix the imaginary problems with his TV or microwave or whatever seemed too *New-Age* and *technical* for him. Even if it took another half hour, she decided, twenty dollars was nothing she could turn down. That'd technically give her a brief hourly wage of $40. Reggie could choke on that next time he teased her too hard.

"Ok," she said. "What you want me to do?"

He actually smiled at her then, the first time he ever seemed pleased with her or like he liked her at all, but she still felt that she was the butt of his inside-but-only-with-himself jokes. The AC was starting to feel like overkill. She had goosebumps.

His hand, as always, was rubbing his triangle, but his hand started to stray—to the left, just a bit, to his *dots*, as Ma called them. His index finger traced it. He probably didn't even realize he was scratching that in front of her, the old coot. Embarrassed for him, Lala looked away.

"You know how your nipples change sometime?" he asked.

"Huh?"

"You know," he said, "like get hard. When you touch em. Or it's cold."

"I guess…"

He chuckled. "She guesses," he said, not to her but not to anybody else either. "She guesses she do. Girly, I know you know what I'm talking about. You've prob-ably discovered that yourself by now, right?"

Lala didn't say anything. This talk was just as strange and undecipherable as anything else he would say—about how *other aliens would weed my yard for less you know* or *your mama is too much of a tightbody to still be single*. And just like when he'd say those things, the things that made her chest a little tight, she waited for him to drop it and give her the money already.

"Alright then," he said.

She scooted to the edge of her seat so she could jump up, get paid, and get out as fast as possible. He might not have a job for her after all.

But he did. At least, kind of. When he finally got to it, his proposition was very simple:

"All you gotta do is pull your top down and show me for ten seconds, and I'll give you the twenty and the five. Easy-peasy. You can even count down the time. But you can't tell anyone, ok? If you be good, we can do this again. Maybe even make it a regular thing. What do you think, honey?"

Lala thought for a minute. It seemed easy enough. She saw something like that on the TV once with Ma— the news was doing a segment on the spring breakers that wrecked through the town every year. An anchor was narrating as the camera panned along the dirty shore and the defiant partiers before stopping on a girl standing in the dunes. She noticed the camera's attention and pulled away her bikini as a response, her chest exploding into a pixelated blur.

Ma laughed then because *that's something me and your auntie would do when we were young and I wasn't yet with your deadbeat but don't you repeat that* and so Lala knew it wasn't that weird. Still, it didn't seem wholly ok. She didn't feel ok.

No. All she had to really say was a single word, but Lala found it was too hard to talk. She shook her head instead. No no no. He just gave a grunt and, to her shock, handed her the twenty and five anyways. She put them in her front pocket.

"Forget about it then, ok?"

Lala nodded, already halfway to the door. He didn't even get up to see her out.

"Think of that as your summer bonus. If your mama ask." His eyes were already back on the TV screen.

As she flew down the driveway, a missed stalk of Bahia grass caught her eye. In one motion, she scooped down, snatched it out of the ground, and did not break her pace until she nearly slammed into her own front door. That's when she noticed just how hard she'd been breathing. The crumpled weed was bleeding a clear sap all over her right palm. She could smell that green stink again.

She dug under the bills to retrieve her key and go inside. And—although she didn't usually do it and didn't have any real reason to do it now—she flipped the top lock up on the door, too. She sat on the cool tile floor and watched 1.5 SpongeBob before she stopped being able to feel her pulse in her fingertips. When it got dark and she'd washed her dinner plates and took a shower, she had to keep the TV on at 24 volume to fall asleep.

She was woken up later that night by Ma's *what in the hell are you trying to lock me out for you little asshole* pounding on the door and she had no answer for why she did it. And when Ma found *another nasty weed La are you trying to bring bugs in*, she had no answer for that, either.

It was a now-distinguishable week later when Lala ran into Reggie, and Reggie did his usual thing where he went at her until she had tears stinging their way out of her eyes, and he laughed and called her *just a little baby brat trying to act so tough*, and then she finally snapped and told him what she thought she'd never say because really it was something to brag about—or at least, that's what she thought.

She didn't even do it, and he still gave her the money. Wasn't that impressive, somehow? Getting that much money from a stupid old man asking stupid questions like that? She came out of it like a fairytale girl outsmarting adults and demons alike.

But then Reggie had her second-guessing. He looked at her like she said Mr. Fred punched her in the face. He started to get mad like she said Mr. Fred had even tried to kill her or something.

"Lala, are you retarded?" he asked.

Only a vocab word from her summer work could describe it: Reggie was *fuming*. And it scared her. And while she didn't know the word he used, the way he said it made her blink tears again. He didn't point it out this time though.

"You don't know what a skeezy geezer is when you see it? He was trying to see your…you know, because he wanted to get off!"

"Get off?" She didn't understand.

"Oh my fucking God," he said. "Like, it makes him horny. Like he wants to do you. He's a pedophile."

Well, she understood that. Suddenly, she thought she understood everything.

He was yelling at her, she figured, the way he wanted to yell at someone else. This was the kind of love that Ma said her *piece of shit father* gave her when they were together, and Lala saw it must have ran on this side of the family. Maybe, Lala thought, maybe Reggie actually didn't mean his meanness after all.

He hunched down so they looked at each other on the same level. She'd never seen his face so serious, so still. His eyes went wide and flashed with anger. So angry, so scary.

But it was for someone else, she had to remind herself. For the skeezy geezer who tried to look at her dots. Reggie seemed ready to kill him. Lala, for whatever reason, felt loved then.

"Lala," he said, "I need you to be straight with me. Did he do anything else?"

"No."

"You sure?"

"Yes."

"He didn't pull his junk out or touch you anywhere?"

"Mm-mm."

"Didn't make you watch any sick shit or film you or anything?"

"No."

"You swear? Nothing else weirder or worse than this?"

"I swear. That's all he asked. And when I said no, he didn't ask again."

"Ok." He stood back up. That's all he needed to hear, she guessed. He didn't say anything else for a minute.

Finally, he said, "Can you come and tell my friends about this?"

Lala went to Reggie's and told Martin and Scamz, and they got just as grossed out and pissed off as he did. So pissed, in fact, that they started to plan. They wanted to *make that old perv pay* and had an idea on how to do it.

Thankfully, they didn't want to tell Ma or the cops or anybody else. They were *gonna have to keep this real secret, like covert operations stuff* to carry out their plan. That made sense. And really, she was just happy that no adults would have to know. She was already embarrassed enough.

They were going to blackmail him. That'd show him. If he would pay a little girl $25 to look at her, they figured he'd pay ten times that to keep them quiet about it. If they could get $250, that'd be $50 each. Not bad for a quick job.

But they thought he might have even more. All their old folk were raised by the Depression—they didn't trust the banks to keep their money safe. If Mr. Fred was like every other old man they knew, then every dollar he ever made was in that house.

They could get hundreds. Thousands, even. If they could find the cash, their shares went up to unfathomable numbers. She'd have to hide it all somehow and she'd have to figure out how to explain to Ma why she avoided his house after, but that all faded when she thought about making maybe even four figures *to-fucking-night*. More cash than she could physically carry. The things she could do with that much money...she couldn't even imagine.

And it was ok, because they were *justified by all accounts and it'd teach him a lesson plus we could shoot him and everybody'd give us a medal anyhow*. So she felt ok about it. She had to—she was going to be the one to get him to open his door at nighttime. They didn't think he'd do it for anybody else. It'd have to be her who went up and knocked on his door while they all waited in the dark behind her and get him in *a tough spot he can't talk his way out of*. Then they'd show him.

With the plan in place, there was nothing left to do but

wait for nightfall. The boys decided to watch *Family Guy* in the meantime. Lala wasn't supposed to watch *stupid violent trash like that*, but it was ok because *well we put it on so it's not like you're doing anything so just chill*, which was the same reasoning used when Martin pulled out a bong and everyone sat around taking deep, dramatic sucks off it. Reggie eventually offered Lala a turn. She copied what they did, doing it so hard she accidentally inhaled water and coughed until her face turned red.

Quickly, though, they taught her how to do it right, and she got high for the very first time, a sinking-type feeling she thought she liked. They all laughed about *the little gangster girl* and she thought she liked that more than anything. For once, she was in on the joke.

On the fourth knock she could hear him shuffling across the tile from the back of the condo to, finally, the front. His figure appeared first in the frosted panel window next to the door, peeping at her, before he was suddenly in front of her. She had a prick of terror as the door opened, realizing that there was nothing left between them now and she was going through with it, but stuffed the fear down. It was surprisingly easy to do that—wiping away emotions —but then she remembered she was high. And that helped.

As she looked at him, she repeated it one more time in her head: he deserved everything coming and it was technically the government's money, anyhow. If she learned anything from Ma and her tax-dodging tactics with her tips, it was that it was ok to *get one over on Uncle Sam every now and then*. It seemed fair.

"You got a watch, girl?" He was only in loose boxers. "You understand how late it is you're coming up here?"

"Yes, sir."

"Well, you got a good reason for it?"

"Um, uh-huh." She fumbled for the lines Reggie gave her. "I figure I owe you."

"Yeah?"

"Yeah. For the money. Cuz I didn't do it. So, I'm here."

"It's a little late for that right now," he said.

But he waved her in. Fighting the lifelong habit, Lala took good care to not lock the door behind her.

She sat on the couch. He went into the kitchen for a minute, for some reason. Then he came over and pulled the chain of the large lamp by the TV, its warm glow casting shadows up to the ceiling. Lala didn't mean to, but she started thinking about the awful fish-monster mask Reggie bought for Halloween that he'd been terrorizing her with ever since. Mr. Fred's face looked just like it now. Creepy. Scary. So ugly and awful she just couldn't stand it.

She could, at least, hear the creaking and shifting of three boys about fifteen feet away outside. It really wasn't that bad because *we're gonna get you outta danger at the last second not that you're in any danger since he probably has dementia* and as soon as she gives the word, they're going to swarm in like the cops.

He sat next to her, his hand falling on her thigh. No adult—not even Ma—ever touched her. Something was wrong with his boxers. She chose to watch her shadow as it climbed and fell on the wall in front of her.

"So," he said, "why the change of heart?"

Lala shrugged. He smiled, nicely, like her doctor did. Patient, kind, like this was his job and he'd seen worse.

"Ok, you don't have to answer. You wanna go ahead then...?"

"Can I...like, wait a moment? I'm...nervous."

The plan was to have a minute of *small talk the way old people always gotta shoot the shit* before she somehow turned the conversation to say something about "Peter." But she never had that chance. She hadn't planned for anything other than what the boys said.

"Nervous?" he repeated. She nodded.

She wasn't even lying—her heart was pounding into her throat. This kind of fear was a first for her.

"Aw," he said. He'd never been soft with her before. "It's ok to be shy. Say, why don't I go first?"

By the time she yelped "Peter," he'd already taken it out. She knew what it was—she'd walked in on Reggie peeing plenty times before—but his penis was swollen and pointing up. It was all too horrific for her to even question. He still had it out when the boys threw open the door and stormed toward the couch.

Reggie lifted Lala up into the air. Martin and Scamz kicked the couch over. Reggie put her down by the door and managed to close it with the weight of her body. The old man hit his head on the ground, hard. She could hear his skull crack against the tile. That was more than enough.

"Fucking perv!" Reggie said.

But Mr. Fred didn't hear him. Martin and Scamz dragged him onto the floor between the living room and kitchen, where most people would have a dining room, to get more room. Mr. Fred's *dirty old dick* was still sticking straight up into the air. Reggie kicked it. Mr. Fred only groaned. Reggie got down and grabbed his face.

"You gotta pay," he said, "or we'll go right to the police."

No!" It came out as more of a gasp than anything else, but it was clear all the same.

"We fucking filmed it, dude! Whole thing's on camera. I'll show everyone if you don't pay up."

Lala didn't know whether that was part of the plan or just a bluff to scare him into submission. She hoped it was just a bluff, maybe as much as Mr. Fred probably hoped it was too. The memory of what was going on was already sinking deep—she could literally feel it cementing right then and there. She didn't need it recorded by others, too.

Real or not, the threat was enough. It took a painfully long time for him to finally tell them where he kept his cash—in the middle drawer of his dresser, somewhere Lala could've guessed. And after only a little more pressing, he admitted that he kept his biggest bills hidden within his late wife's coats in the bedroom closet.

They sent Lala to go get those. There was more noise, noise she tried to hum out, while she went into his bedroom and got out one, two, three, four, five, six, seven…twenty hundred-dollar bills and a thin little brochure thing from two scratchy church jackets and one dark green windbreaker.

The brochure was actually one of those pamphlets they give out at a funeral. From the dim light that reached back into the bedroom from under the closed door, Lala could see a young woman smiling stiffly on the front. She looked like she was only enduring the photographer to get it over with. Her death date was twelve years ago and "unexpected," according to the two-paragraph biography. Her parents were still alive or, at least, they were alive when she died. Mr. Fred's real name was Frederick. Weird.

Lala thought for a minute. Twenty times one hundred is two thousand, an unbelievable sum that far exceeded their expectations. But it wasn't really theirs. The boys, that is. What'd they even do? If she'd been a little smarter, Lala could have done this on her own. And she wouldn't have had to beat him up, either. Now they were being just as bad as him.

So the boys had to pay like Mr. Fred, she figured. But just a little. She deserved more than just an even-Steven split. She had to put up with him the most, so she should get the most. It was only fair.

Leaving seven hundred was still way more than any of them thought they could get. She made the thirteen fit without any lumps in the top of her shirt. It had a built-in training bra *to get you used to that awful cage you'll need soon oh I'm just kidding now it's really fine*, so the bills were compressed and didn't show whatsoever. Not that anybody—else—would want to be looking there, anyways.

She stuffed the pamphlet back into a coat pocket

and walked out into the living room. She kept her left hand extended so that the $700 was as far away from her body as possible, the bills held out like an offering to the feral young men that were only just now starting to lose steam. Scamz kicked Mr. Fred half-heartedly, his foot barely even touching. When they saw her—and the money—they stopped completely.

"He's not…?" Lala asked, the unspoken word heavy in the air.

Martin looked unsure. Scamz and Reggie looked like they didn't care. Mr. Fred laid like a KO'd villain in the thriller movies: not dead, but not getting up anytime soon. They all just shrugged.

"Nah," Reggie finally decided, "he'll be fine."

Then he grabbed the bills from her, counted them out, shook his head once in surprise, and whistled. He shoved the fistful deep into his front pocket.

"I'll distribute it back home," he said. "Let's clean up and go."

The boys righted the couch and worked together to gently lift Mr. Fred back onto it. His eyes fluttered. His head bled. But the worst damage was inflicted on his middle. She could already see shoeprints blooming red all over his distended old-man belly.

Martin grabbed a little throw blanket off the bed and covered him with it while Scamz and Reggie wiped drops of blood and potential fingerprints with paper towels they got in the kitchen. If the cops went forensic on the scene, there was no way they were going to get away with this.

"Hey."

Reggie turned her away from the couch and

toward him. He'd never seemed so much older than her as he did then. Lala realized just how quickly and completely puberty aged him. It was like he'd gone through an accelerator—one minute the wispy-stached jerk whose voice cracked when he mocked her, the next a man with facial hair and muscles that shone with the sweat he'd worked up under the lamplight. It seemed to happen right here, right now. Lala wondered how, once she'd jumped through that portal too, she would turn out. And whether this night would hopefully make it happen.

"Hey, Lala," he said, "chill out, ok? It's all good. Ok?"

His shoes were stained. Mr. Fred's labored breathing made the room unbearably loud. Still, she nodded. He squeezed her shoulder. He was way too much like an adult now.

There was only a brief collective moment of panic when they realized they couldn't lock the door behind them. If anyone came, they might realize that someone had to have been there. But then they figured *old people leave their doors unlocked all the time so it's probably fine* and they had to just accept that.

Nobody looked back at what they left there. Whatever was going to happen with that, they had about three days, maybe less if Ma had any questions. Reggie and Lala had to keep up with the lawn like normal. If anybody asked, they would shrug it off and say something like *I thought maybe he was trying to dodge paying me* or along those lines. Now more than ever, they had to act normal.

And they couldn't go blowing cash, either. At

Reggie's house, they learned they each earned $175. Lala was surprised when the boys each took a small cut out of theirs to give her $200 *since you had got us there in the first place*, an enormously generous gesture that made her almost feel bad about what she had hidden from them. But she knew better—boys will be boys and can rely on violence, but girls must be clever. This was how she'd have to survive.

They'd all never had so much money before. There were so many ways to spend it—when the coast was clear, of course. For now, the boys were hiding it with their weed. Then, one day, they might get new video games and band shirts, skater shoes and alcohol from even older boys, black-market knives and maybe even *a handy from loose Brenda if I ask nice enough*. They were getting almost hysterical with possibilities.

Lala stayed quiet. She was thinking about where she'd be able to hide this much money from Ma and what she'd be able to get without suspicion. Candy from the bodega. New pencils from the school bookstore. Maybe, maybe, a sundress so popular with girls her age at the mall.

Ma wasn't exactly paying close attention, but she wasn't stupid. Ironically, it was starting to seem that having a lot of illicit money caused as many problems for her as having very little legitimate money did. Such a common thought, but she got it now. She was learning a lot lately.

Now that they'd gotten what they wanted from her, the boys wanted her gone. Just as well—Lala wanted out. It was almost 10 PM. Ma would probably be home soon. She had a lot to do, and she couldn't do any of it here. Plus, Reggie's room reeked. The smell was making her head throb.

Though there wasn't a thing left in the world to be afraid of, Reggie still insisted on walking her home. They didn't talk much. Weirdly, he hugged her when they got to the door.

"Take care, prima," he said. He tried to say it cool, but she heard the fear warbling in the back of his throat. "We're family, you know. I'm always gonna look out for you. But you gotta look out for me now, ok? You can't say nothing."

"I know." He was standing too close.

"You're not feeling like, bad or nothing?"

"No."

"For real?"

"Yeah."

"Damn." He laughed with relief. "You're cold, little cuz. But I like that. Just don't be cold to me."

"I won't."

With one more look, he turned and walked back down the street. Lala went in and got ready for bed, leaving every light off in the process. Ma would later complain *you're like a little bat whatever but can you at least leave one god damn lamp on for me* but she always seemed to find something to complain about, so Lala didn't take it too seriously. She wouldn't get in trouble.

She never really did.

* * *

Nothing much happened with Mr. Fred. Lala saw an ambulance parked in his driveway a day or two later. Ma was driving them to the grocery store, so she didn't see more than that. The EMTs were probably inside at the time.

Ma didn't comment on it. The ambulance. She might not have noticed. When Lala later asked, as casually as she could, about what happened to Mr. Fred as Ma was getting ready for work, she didn't even stop.

"Oh, I heard he had a fall."

She was upside-down gathering her hair into a high ponytail. She flipped back up and snapped the elastic in place.

"It's really common with elderly people, especially when they live alone. I hope they get him in a nursing home or something."

"Is he coming back? Like, am I still going to weed his lawn and stuff?"

"I don't know, honey. I think it's safe to say you're probably out of a job. Sorry."

"That's ok." Lala knew it'd be suspicious to say she hoped he was ok or whatever, so she left it at that.

"Maybe you could ask around, see if anybody has anything else for you?"

Lala nodded and left Ma alone. She obviously didn't need the work but later in the summer, when the unsupervised days stretched like agony in front of her, she finally broke and started walking small dogs around the neighborhood. She made way more doing that than she ever did from Mr. Fred. Fuck his $5 a week—Lala was making $5 per dog per *day*.

She started making enough that Ma let her open up a junior bank account with her. After that first appointment, Lala went back to break her hundreds up into twenties. While she couldn't put it all away then, smaller bills were much easier to move.

She divided them into several hiding spots: taped under the bed, tucked in the back of her math workbook, zipped into the cushion of the reading chair, and a small amount folded under the base of her lamp. If one stash should be discovered, the rest would at least be there. She risked as little as possible and tried to cut her losses as much as she could. Lala was, above all things, pretty shrewd for her age.

Once a month for the next two years, Lala walked to the bank and deposited 75% of what she made the month before, plus an extra $20 from her secret stash. If Ma ever asked, she'd just tell her it was a generous tip from a neighbor she didn't know. This kind of laundering was much slower and much less exciting than the mafioso stuff, but it was the only way she'd get away with it. She was sure of that.

Lala never saw Mr. Fred again. She never saw cops at his condo, or strange family members either. She did see a new family move in a few months later, though. Perhaps they'd bought the place with everything still inside. It was like he'd been completely and cleanly erased from ever being there. And Lala was happy to leave it that way.

Reggie never talked about it. The teasing stopped. When they saw each other, it was brief. Few words were ever exchanged, sometimes no more than a nod. They didn't have that much in common after all.

Reggie turned out to be a *deadbeat just like him see* by seventeen when he got sentenced to five years in an adult prison for assault with a deadly weapon. That is, he stabbed another kid in a fight. He didn't die. The knife did only minor damage, all things considered. It could have been worse.

Even though she was old enough at this point to see what the inside of a prison looked like, Ma screamed at Tia Jana in the driveway when she tried to come invite Lala to visit with her. So Lala never went. She probably didn't want to, anyways.

Once, just before that whole *public fucking Maury- like confrontation,* Lala went to take a twenty from the stash in her old workbook to the bank when she discovered half was missing. The money couldn't have fallen out—Lala kept it paperclipped to the page. She was down about $150.

Instead, there was a sticky-note. It was from her own stationery, a large blue note with a white kitten at the bottom. In her overly neat script, Ma had written:

IOU $150 <3

But she never paid Lala back. Of course Lala never asked for it, either. She let it go immediately. Just to be safe, she changed out her hiding spots and upped her monthly deposit to $25. It never happened again.

* * *

By the end of high school, Lala was working in a fancy seaside restaurant like Ma. She had enough in savings to cover the first year of tuition without any financial aid, but she wasn't going to college. At least not yet. The world was coming alive with money now—there was no sense wasting it to keep sitting in a classroom and miss out.

Because Lala was a pretty young woman with a sweet mouth and actual breasts now, men tipped 30-200% on top of their already overpriced meals. They would look right at her body as they said stuff about *that figure good golly you could be a movie star but really I'd hope you'd be in dirty movies* and this time, Lala would let them. They would do it anyhow. This way, she was at least making it worth her while.

She wasn't stupid. She needed a degree to get out of her trashy little beach town, she knew that. She wasn't gonna be like Ma: always on her feet, always unhappy. This was not a forever thing.

She would go to college, eventually. But there was no need to rush. She figured she'd spend a few years stacking the chips so when she did go, she could move somewhere fancy and take a couple years off of work while she studied. The money she'd have built up, she wouldn't have to limit her options for the sake of in-state tuition. Maybe she'd get a marketing degree in Chicago or go to an entrepreneurship program in California. She always had a mind for business, or so she'd been told.

For now, she'd keep working and keep saving. And maybe have a little fun after-hours, too. No harm in that. The head bartender wasn't going to derail her plans. Neither would the occasional bump, just to get through double shifts.

Vices—indulged only sparingly—could not distract her. Sometimes, she figured, they were there to help her avoid burnout. That posed a real risk in a job like this. So the ends justified the means justified the check justified the job. Whatever helped keep her going.

Lala was going to make it. And she had plenty of time.

Lala had only ever talked about what happened with Mr. Fred once. She had been seeing her first pseudo-boyfriend, a situation that she'd find would repeat itself far too many times. This one, though, ended of her own accord.

They were sitting on his couch. She was trying to make sense of the last twenty minutes of a movie they hadn't watched in good faith. He had given up completely. He wanted to talk instead. And because he was still high but no longer horny, he wanted to have some deep conversation.

"What's the worst thing you've ever done?"

This was his best attempt at some profound, probing question to unlock her. She sighed and paused the movie.

"I killed an old pervert."

"No, like really."

"Really, though."

He sat up and looked at her for a long time. Panic hit her in the stomach, and she added:

"Well, I shouldn't say killed. My cousin and his friends beat him up because I told them about him."

He still didn't say anything. Realizing how it sounded, she then said:

"I wasn't molested, though. He just flashed me. That's all."

He reached over and touched her arm. Then, he bent over to kiss the top of her left hand. He looked up at her, his eyes like those of a dog begging for food. Lala didn't understand.

"I am so sorry that happened to you," was all he said.

After that, he treated her too much like some fragile thing, like a little victim in need of help. He spoke to her in a coaxing, theatrically gentle voice and always kept a protective hand on the small of her back. He stopped offering her coke and *just wanted to see if you needed to talk* if she so much as knocked back a drink during close.

Sex became tedious—too much asking for permission, too many stops and starts, too often he'd check *please let me know if you're not alright ok* and it all just became too obnoxious for her. The whole thing seemed to affect him more. He couldn't fulfill his role anymore: couldn't share lines, couldn't call her out for being bitchy to good-tipping men, couldn't so much as lightly slap her. And he couldn't make her cum. She broke things off shortly after.

Lala never told anyone again. She wouldn't make that mistake twice. But if she ever did, she'd at least hope they would react differently. He had mistaken her for a girl who'd had something done to her, for prey. But Lala wasn't that. What she'd wanted—if she was honest with herself—was for him to have seen her as a predator, too. In her own right. Maybe.

Ok, maybe not a predator. She'd never do anything

unprovoked. Maybe she was just a girl who did her best with what she was given. Like all things, she figured out how to make it work for her. That much had to be respected.

Lala only ever wore low-cut tops and endured pervy comments when she was on the clock. She agreed to sex-only arrangements because that's what she wanted. Once she knew those boys well enough, she'd be the one putting their hands around her throat. She was always starting things, setting the situation. It was always within her control. It was always her.

DAMNED IN D3

Might as well smoke. Might as well smoke as much as he damn well pleased. What did it matter? Lung cancer wasn't gonna get him quicker than what he was about to do. He found himself smiling as he tapped another cigarette out of her carton. There was no such thing as indulgences right before death, he figured. Get it while you can, baby.

She was the one that liked menthols. Oh well. Menthols were too much like her for his taste. But menthols, smeared at the tip with the dried brown of her blood, was the best he could do for the moment.

Marie. Marie was right where he'd seen her last— still smirking at him from the bed. He beat the sadistic flash out of her eyes with a wooden rod from the headboard, but even sans life, this woman was giving him the run for it.

What did she expect, really? Deprive a man of intimacies for months, allot him twenty almost painful minutes, and then tell him you've been sleeping with his best friend and you weren't sorry, oh never sorry because *I've wasted ten of my best years living with a mockery of a man and I might as well sleep with the whole town and everybody'll know John, oh from the grocer to the—*

Of course he was going to react. Really.

But this was her game, this had always been her game. She'd always wanted to see to it that he suffered for her. She made him love her when she wasn't supposed to be loved—lithe little thing eyeing her professor up and down and all around, got him fired and nearly arrested. She made good and sure that the whole student body knew she got him that way.

And she even had to make sure the rest of the world knew, too. *He was actually my professor. Until his cock got hard!* That was her favorite fact to drop at parties, the quickest cut she could make that made others look at him with disgust. She often made women gasp—literally, audibly gasp—and walk away without so much as an *if you excuse me I need to go see about something in the kitchen* excuse.

He couldn't be surprised when he stopped receiving invitations to so much as a small dinner party. She made quick work of his social standing with that vulgar little mouth of hers. On their first anniversary, he had nobody to celebrate with, aside from her. By their second anniversary, they'd gone fifteen months without the phone ringing and almost ten months without anyone answering.

Could've made new friends, sure. Could've done a lot of things, but he definitely could've struck up a conversation with the loud Irishmen who came straight to the bar from their dirty factory jobs and sat with his illiterate coworkers in the break room rather than self-segregate with his paperbacks. He could've deigned himself to rougher company, because it was company all the same, but then that felt too much admitting just how far he had fallen for this woman, this woman he didn't even want to look at.

She was all he had. She had her little shopgirl sluts, but Marie was the master of his needs: sex, sustenance, speak. He was simple. And yet, she made it difficult. Fucking difficult.

When they fought—which, if you can imagine, was all the time—every neighbor in the tenement would hear her call him a *dirty old man who can't even get off because I'm not a little girl anymore*. Made him out into some monster, Marie did.

Took him and pushed him and sometimes made him so desperately weak for her that they both ended here in a ratshit apartment. Marie, he supposed, had tired of the game. *She* ended it exactly this way. Not him. She wanted the hard wood to splinter her brains —not him.

And of course, she wanted him to lose like this. That was her game. She never wanted to win so much as she wanted to make him lose. She was good at that, making men like him lose. To dare to meet Marie's pseudo-sweet gaze, to kiss those poisoned-sugar lips, was to lose everything.

"And," he said to the newfound stillness between them, "I guess I've known it all along."

Right. Something he could swallow, something he could slice. Take two breaths and embrace the black. He rose from his chair, flicked the puckering embers onto the floor, and turned his eyes back toward dear Marie's way.

Her crushed skull and wide-open mouth were both so wet and shiny with blood. Even like this, she could still beckon him further to his demise. He leaned over and pressed his lips against her bottom one, the one least damaged by her act.

Back up again. Find a method in the bathroom. She probably had left something for him to find in the bathroom. The last steps seemed so clear to him.

But something surprising here: a laugh. This, she did not plan for. He began to laugh, laugh, laugh. Almost cried with laughter at the whole thing.

He wasn't going to take it that far.

PIG PEACE

For as much time as I hung around Aidie's place, the shrieks still brought my hands up to cover my ears, my eyes blinking hard in fright. I tried to play it off, but Aidie never let me.

"It's just their nervous system's response," she'd say.

You'd think she'd be rolling her eyes as she said it, but she was really trying to comfort me in her own Miss Bitch way.

"You don't need to get all freaked out like that."

And while yes, yes *ma'am*, I knew that better than anyone, it wasn't something I could control. Their nervous systems responded to the bullets tearing through their bodies and my nervous system responded in kind.

Sometimes they didn't make much noise. Sometimes only Jeff did, shouting out to no one in particular that *I got 'em good!* Getting 'em good meant making a shot in their lungs, which instantly took the breath out of them, followed by everything else.

If we were close we could hear them, their useless sucking of air and gurgling on the forest floor as Jeff laughed and already started tying up their limbs. These were things, needless to say, that I wasn't wanting to hear. I'd breathe hard or hum or make my ears rumble but it never covered up the noise.

"Circle of life, Clem," Aidie always said. "You have a big heart and that's beautiful, but we need to eat too."

They really did eat the hogs, at least. It's the only meat Aidie ate. She didn't believe in buying store-made bacon or burger when she knew the horrors those animals went through from start to finish. The hogs hanging around their property only had a few bad minutes at the end.

Aidie was never the one to be ending them when that time came. But she made them. Not the way she made me, the way she picked out an unmothered girl from her fifth grade class and insisted her friendship upon me, the way she loved me so hard that I couldn't imagine any life without it forever and ever and even after. She *made* them, the way a mother makes a child. I'll explain.

I'm pretty sure I remember the first time. It was the summer between our junior and senior year, a claustrophobic period that movies make out as the *times of our lives* but then they'd never spent summer in a beachless middle-of-nowhere Florida town. Florida is only fun when you have money; the adults could barely get even minimum-wage jobs here. The good town of Pantano offered us nothing more than tedium, the kind that makes its children turn to drugs and alcohol. But we didn't have that. Not really. Not yet.

We passed that stretch of flat, hot days sweating it out in Aidie's Florida Room, leafing through old magazines her mother once had and talking those aimless talks about how *we're gonna make it out of here* and *fuck this place* and all that. Sometimes Aidie went out. Usually I would stay. Jeff didn't care. Jeff thought of me *like another little sister* and he wasn't too weird about it.

One afternoon, Aidie went out. I stayed. I was halfway through a 50s teenybopper magazine when

Aidie came back with a man, maybe fifty-five. I never learned his real age. In any case, he could've been her father, had her father not been locked up for shooting her mother.

He didn't kill her though, which was honestly even worse—her mom was more or less what we called a vegetable back then (sorry!). Jeff had taken her from the hospital to an invalid home after it happened. I waited outside the room when Aidie visited her for the first and final time. It was one of those brutal places where someone screamed nonstop and every inhale had a little whiff of shit. But Aidie said it made no difference since *it's not like she fucking knows what's going on anyway.*

Anyway. The guy. He came in holding Aidie's hand but she was walking ahead, leading the way like a schoolteacher would with an embarrassed little boy. But he had one of those shit-eating, *I'm fucking* type of grins.

"This is Jim," Aidie said. "Jim, this is my friend."

"Hi girlie," he said. I dropped the magazine on to my chest.

"She's not coming with us." Aidie turned back and used her free hand to I guess preemptively smack him in the check. "Just to get that out of the way."

"Well that's fine." Now he smacked her ass. "Your daddy isn't home, is he?"

I saw the smile she was biting on and knew just about what she'd say. She got a weird thrill out of it that I would never admit I understood.

"No, but when he gets home he'll shoot you. But

he ain't coming home for 25 to life, so we don't gotta worry."

"Huh."

"Now say goodbye to my friend here."

To that he lifted up one hand, wiggled his fingers at me.

"Now Clem, you say goodbye to Jim."

"Bye." I brought my magazine back up to my face. "Jim."

I didn't watch them walk away. For the next hour, I force-focused my eyes on the page and tried not to hear any of the mess going on a few rooms down. There were too many questions that Aidie would never answer, questions I was too scared to even breach.

First, what the fuck? I mean, we never bought into that *chewed gum* bullshit, but I figured Aidie would spend her virginity on someone at least in our school, if only to make the semester more interesting. And who the fuck was this guy? He should've looked familiar but he didn't. Everybody knew everybody in this three-digit total population town and this was a face I had never seen before, except maybe on a Wanted poster. He looked like something dangerous, like the Misfit of the only O'Connor story we read in school. Strangers didn't come here, not even on their way to somewhere else.

She really went out, caught an unknown, and brought him back here to…what, exactly? Throw him onto her twin bed, pull down her cutoffs, and pierce herself on him? That's the only way that made sense, her mounting him. I could picture it so clear I might as well've been involved after all.

I didn't want to, but I could even see his atrophied penis—something that, once presented, Aidie would laugh and think, *And that's what all the fuss is about?* Some little pecker peeking out under the beer gut. Lord. That's the first thing I had noticed about him, the beer gut. His abdomen looked almost a little pregnant, if it hadn't have been hanging so low. It looked like the start of ascites.

I learned about that with my dad. That was 1–1 on shitty and dead or otherwise unavailable fathers, by the way, and even we understood that was half of why we so stubbornly clung to each other.

It sounded like she was enjoying herself, at least. He certainly was—squeals of something like delight and an enthusiastic bump-bump of the bed against the wall. Or someone banging the wall. It sounded more than pornographic. Even the neon-lidded women on Jeff's tapes gave a more subtle performance.

No jazz-lite score to accompany this afternoon, either. Just the continued banging, his grunting, the occasional burst of melody out her mouth. Over and over but not rhythmically so. Oh.

Reading—if you could call it that—was impossible. Visions of damp pubic hair swam across a spread of the '53 Junior Miss Fall Fashions, tangling in their little pearl chokers, spread like moss under kitten-heeled feet. Lurking behind smiling ladies in a department store advert was, again, that horrible penis. A one-page feature on June Allyson and her nondescript Frankish smile—and that pale-blue organ again.

I was riding the last gasp of a high or else it would have occurred to me to just go outside. But I was still scared of the wild hogs that roamed the property, an invasion that had only just begun in nowhere Florida. A case of a few farm pigs getting loose, supposedly.

Only one generation to transform from domesticity, they said. Only a few wild years until hair grows and hides darken and teeth come in nice and long and sharp as soon as their bodies learn they have to fend for themselves. The brutal magic of the Everglades can swallow up little pink piggies and work them over into monsters, and then give those monsters the cover to multiply.

The occasional mama hog and little baby hoglets seen snortling around the roads mostly aroused just a passive pity. Even schoolchildren understood they would probably have to be shot and felt somehow worse about that than what it took to get Miss Pink Piggy on their plate. The latter happened in some other place, so it didn't really happen at all. Here you couldn't make it to ten years old without seeing the kindly senior Mr. Jenkins enact the alternative ending of *Wilbur* on his front lawn. Or your friend's brother using a shovel in the worst way.

Anyway. It was the massive male hogs—boars— that made for the stuff of horror movies. You can nod and say, "I totally get it," but you really never will, not until you've been in breathing distance of one. Boars are just one big fucking muscle of dumb righteous hatred for us. They will kill you if you let them.

But they are beautiful, in that terrifying God's-fuckup-and-forsaken kind of way. Every time a penis ends up in my mouth, a boar will flash across my eyes. And I think: *Bristle. Foreskin. Hooves. Scrotum. Maw. Frenulum.*

Just as I was starting to think this was in fact an elaborate prank—I couldn't put something like that past Aidie—the air fell silent. I looked up, for some reason. I heard a door opening, quick heavy steps trotting out. Then, I heard the door pulled closed and locked both ways.

"Clem?" Her voice grew louder as she made her way toward me. "I'm done now."

"What…?"

But there was too much to ask. So I just didn't. And she didn't offer anything, not really. Instead she just held up a pair of crumpled white cotton panties, trimmed with scalloped lace and patterned with little gray daisies. And a little blood.

"Look." She wore the same smile she had when she won the fifth-grade spelling bee. "I actually bled."

The panties went up like a flag on a post in the backyard. What victory there was to display, I don't know, but Jeff said we ought to do this every day *because I swear this shit calling all the hogs on over so's I can send them off to Hog Heaven*. Two peas in a panty, I guess. Though I didn't correct him that she was the only one doing it, not me.

She didn't bring another man over for a couple weeks. The next time, I was more freshly high and she left the door open during it. I thought I caught a peek of something when I crept to the bathroom and back. I saw flesh for sure, maybe some shapes. But it wasn't my business, I didn't think. I did not linger.

The next next time, Aidie brought another stranger who promised *double if you sit with us and maybe just touch it a little*. I asked Aidie if we could step aside a moment. I found myself asking the man that too, my sweet-girl schooling overriding all other instincts. I might as well have curtsied as we went outside to talk.

"Are you a hooker?" I asked her. "Is that what this has been?"

"I haven't been paid a single red cent." Aidie said it proudly. Her peaches-and-cream face was flushed strawberry with excitement.

She leaned in to whisper, "Do you trust me?"

"Trust for what?"

"Me."

She leaned in even closer, closer, and then pulled back just as I realized she'd kissed me. Then she laughed like she'd just pantsed me instead. But then she grabbed my hand.

"Clem, if I ask you to, will you come in and just do what I say and know that nothing bad is going to happen? I would never let anyone hurt you."

"I mean I do, but—"

"I want to show you something. Something I can't show anyone else."

I let her lead me into the bedroom, sit me down in her worn-out beanbag, and show me what went on. It was as I imagined. She asked if I would touch it. I did, for a second. She didn't push anything else. I sat and watched and very very briefly *yeah stroke my hog girl you got this* held it in my hand like a dying rat pup and tried to detach, look passive-like like it was one Jeff's tapes glowing on the TV in the dark dark hours of night.

But it wasn't. No edits, no lighting, no soundtrack, no direction. Just a lot of awkward moving around and one of those beach-burnt white men with a barb wire tattooed around the circumference of his thigh. Leg hair that looked darker and coarser than when he first took off his pants. Feet—

"Clem, do you want to go or do you want to stay?"

She could've been asking me this at a lake party that had begun to falter. Aidie looked down from the bed at me: all casual, no fear. His eyes—shrinking even still behind a growing snout—were alit with greed. Glee. However that saying goes.

There was an answer trapped up in my throat, burping to the surface in just one consonant: "I…uh… I…" Not speech, not enough. I wasn't even sure quite where it was going.

"You just sit there and tell me when you've had enough, okay?"

I couldn't. So I did. And she turned back and kept him moving right along. When he'd finished, she opened the front door for him and he went right through and out into the woods.

"See?" she asked. Not like, *did you see what just happened* because that was obvious. I saw everything. She meant more like, *that wasn't so bad now was it*. I didn't even know what I felt.

She was making two mayo-and-tomato sandwiches in only her shorts. He'd shredded her shirt, but then that was her *fault for leaving it on the floor*.

"He's going to be so happy out there. It's just better

for everyone. We don't need them running wild, not those men."

"How do you know?" I asked.

I had to keep my tongue buffered between my two rows of teeth, or else they would chatter. I'd only experienced bruxism—that's the clinical term for it—once before in my life, when I found my father in his trailer.

"How do you know they deserve this?"

Aidie cut my sandwich diagonally and handed me the first half. Despite myself, I ate it immediately. I was fucking hungry.

"Oh, my darling Clem-en-tine," Aidie sang. She was the only one I had ever confirmed to that yes, actually, I was named for the stupid fucking song. "Any man his age who wants to fuck a girl my age is a man not worth living, at least not with their dicks and hands and everything else they use. It's not like I'm bringing them back here and killing them."

It was like the rest of that sentence dropped into the air as soon as her mouth closed: *not directly*. She looked at me with guiltless eyes and handed me the other half of my sandwich. I took it. I ate. We did not speak further on it.

I didn't stop it. I didn't know what to stop—not that it's much of an excuse, really. I could have tried. Instead I just nodded when she left, gave a quick hello when they came back, and put on a record when they went to her room.

I didn't want to look at the men, but I saw them anyhow: Sunshine State trash with tans like a hide, smiles dotted with dead and rotting teeth, greasy hair styled in mullets or combed back into ponytails the size of smoke wisps or clotted across a see-through scalp. Men, bad men, men who were ugly in that way that did not make me question the sentence Aidie had brought upon them.

I could only look at those men in quick cutting glances, then look back at my book as they walked away. As June dragged toward July, I had finally acquiesced to my summer reading and began to work through a small stack from the library. I slogged my way through *Heart of Darkness* during Mark and half of Jack, and *Of Mice and Men* during the other half of Jack, Dick, Robert, and Tom. I saved the worst for last and when that due date pressed on me, *Jane Eyre* proved a bitch, taking all of Bob, Willie, Bill, Liam, and a one-armed man who called himself Bobby-Boy. Now, whenever I hear a mention of these books or see some other bored student clutching those covers, the men come back to me. I don't remember the stories so much as the transformations that took place within our home as I read them.

Not that it was all we did, though. Not all. Sometimes we went out, taking flip-flopped walks to tread water in the spring, to try to score dope (like grass, not smack) on Main Street, to smoke that dope out in the scrub, to steal snacks from my mom's place when she was at work, to shoplift makeup at the grocery store when she wasn't at work, then back to the lake, then repeat the pathetic triangle of destinations we had in that nothing town.

Boredom in those days was like a school made of small fish; easy to dispel with a little movement, but the moment you're still, it comes creeping back in from all sides, converging into one dark mass at your ankles, slipping between your toes. When the boredom seemed to chase us from spot to spot, we just decided to *fuck it all and go home, ok?* Sometimes we'd hitchhike the way back. And it was on some of those times that we met Bob, Dick, and Jack.

Home was not a proper-noun Home, not until it was time to climb into Aidie's bed and sleep like huddled cave animals, not a Home except when her warm skin was touching mine. There was no air to breathe in, not when so many boars roamed outside and Jeff stretched out on the sofa in his torn boxers.

Some days struck us with restlessness, days that drove us from here to here to here, trying to find somewhere to so much as lay down as the claustrophobia of the great green vasts closed in on us. Nowhere did we find whatever it was we needed, not there.

Time yawned, and out from its great mouth stretched these days. Days and days eternal, days punctuated only by our men: by Garett, by Frank, by Eric, by Dan, by Elijah, by some others whose names were never said or quickly forgotten. I started not to remember them all, or else not to know.

And it's kind of funny, because it's some of these later ones that I watched and *if she's not gonna touch me then why don't y'all at least show me what good friends you are*. Those times, me and Aidie as an act and then eventually me and Aidie alone, will be the times I try coming home to when death calls for me. Everything else was just the details to a book I barely read.

Finally, finally, it was the Fourth of July. This was the holiday our town was best at, a day of rednecks brought to a fever pitch that the heat brought on. Town folk would revel in our delirium and call it patriotic, gathering at the spring for fireworks on the shore and meth in the parking lot. Alcohol allowed teens to roll together in truck beds and made men collide over petty nothings already forgotten by the time the first fist flies.

This time was the first in living memory that the holiday passed without a death to round out the night. Other years saw some kid drowning in the spring, drunken crashes that threw passengers clear through the windshield, someone catching a bullet over drugs or a woman, or occasionally an overdose that would lay undiscovered until the morning. I used to think I was clever to connect these pointless holiday deaths to Shirley's Jackson lottery story we read in school, but I could never quite articulate why.

It wasn't yet night and we were each already six beers deep. We'd tied the typical red-white-and-blue ribbons at the end of our *like a farmgirl but only as a joke you know* braids and one of Aidie's had fallen off. The ribbon that is, not her braid. We stumbled around in the sand, giggling, as we tried to find it. Instead we found a boy crying in an ever-darkening spot on the shore.

I knew him—knew him well, actually. Ike Allito. He was a couple years younger than me, but still younger enough that I used to babysit him. Another daddy-less boy who had more kin inside prison than out, but he was always real *yes ma'am* to me and all that. Aidie saw him, stopped in her teeter-tottering tracks, and started toward where he sat. And I came following behind.

"You alright there?" Aidie bent down and put a hand on his shoulder. "It's not safe to be all by yourself, you know."

Ike lifted his head, his overgrown hair falling over one eye. The other still had those long, straight lashes that stuck straight down, like a cow's eye. He had swallowed the stifled little sobs when he saw us and and now his chest heaved as if he were holding back a cough, like he was trying not to alarm anyone to some hidden illness. He looked at us with his one light pink-rimmed cow eye and bit at his dark pink mouth, the colors you get from crying, and breathed shakily through his red red nose.

"Hi Clementine," he said, and managed a small smile. "I'm ok."

"Are you sure?" It was me asking this time. And it was obvious, of course. Couldn't be too good, crying like that. Ike shrugged.

"Just…some of the boys suck, is all."

"I get that," Aidie said, her mouth curled open. A bright pop of fireworks gleamed in the reflection of her wet teeth.

"'Hell is other people,'" I offered. Nobody took it.

Beer, then. It was the only way we knew how to make the boy feel better. I guess we weren't really any smarter than the people around us. But it worked.

By the time the sun had gone out and the fireworks started in earnest, Ike's troubles had long been forgotten and we were playing Sea Monsters in the water like children. I knew I was *three sheets to the wind* because not once did I give a shit that there might be a gator lurking underneath, that there probably was a gator. They just weren't worth my attention, let alone my fear.

Everything was fine until it wasn't. Or maybe it was fucked from the moment it all started. But it was for sure fucked when Aidie froze mid-splash at something that happened below the surface. Ike had been play-attacking her, "catching" her way more gently than Jeff ever did. As soon as she froze, he immediately let go and swam some distance away from her. I could only see their faces in the short bursts of the fireworks and I was just a little too far away to hear. The whole thing played out like a silent vignette with shadow puppets—without much extra detail, but clearly enough. Transgression.

For a moment there were only the booms and cicadas, the still water between us. I thought about breaking the tension or else acting like nothing happened, but I couldn't make myself do it. It was like being stuck in a dream—my body went heavy in the water, my mouth fixed shut. Slowly, they both got out. Even slower still, I got out too.

I joined Aidie over where we had left our shorts and shoes. Ike went to finish his last beer a couple yards away. Aidie leaned in to whisper over the fireworks what he had done.

"I thought I caught him looking down both our bikinis," she said. "And you know, whatever. But then when he brushed his fucking boner up against me in the spring—God! He's gonna be just like his brothers."

"Aidie."

"I know. Listen though, you know what they are all about, don't you?"

Of course I did: date rape, domestic violence, double homicide. Ike was the latest in a long line of *bad motherfucking boys that you might as well shoot out the womb* and he would probably prove no exception. Probably. But I knew where Aidie was already headed and I wouldn't go there, couldn't go there.

"He's a kid."

"So are we." Aidie didn't even blink. A firework exploded behind her in the distance and for a second, the golden sparks made a violent crown above her head. "And not for long, anyhow."

"Aidie."

"'*Aidie.*' And?"

"You can't decide something like that on what they might do. It's not fair."

At this Aidie laughed, but she laughed like I had been flirting with her. She laced her arms around my neck, her fingers tickling my back. So this was how she would lure me in if I was a man. This is exactly how she would do it.

"Clem." I could feel the gentle pulls of her hand in my hair. I didn't look at her. "You know I love you more than anyone, don't you?"

I did. And I knew that all those things she thought about Ike, they were probably true. I didn't think he meant to put himself on her, but I didn't doubt he did it. When he was little I once caught him hiding in the shower to watch me pee. Hoglets and shovels.

A volley of Roman Candles soared through the air, popping closer than any firework had. Aidie put her hands to her ears and screamed, and then winced in embarrassment. There was more than one reason why we had been so far away from the party.

"You alright?" Ike called out from his spot on the beach. He had helped himself to a fresh beer and held the other spent one in his left hand.

"I'm fine," she called back. To me she said, "I'm sorry. It's when I don't know they're coming."

And it was in that moment that I loved her more than I ever could again, the love only teens or mothers are capable of. It terrified me. She made me move my own limits and I knew why. I knew that I would always love Aidie more than I would ever love a man, more than I would ever love anyone else.

I knew too that she was twisted beyond belief. Some would call a creature like that evil. And as I sat facing the water, drinking what I swore to be my last beer of the night while Aidie guided Ike sweetly into the trees, I knew that maybe I was evil too.

Aidie'd been home when her father went crazy, you know. He chased her around with a shotgun until she managed to get out to the backyard. She told the police that her mother had been shot while helping Aidie escape. She only told me that really, her mom had walked around the house as it all happened without so much as a *get away from her*, and Aidie had to plead with her from outside to *come on Mama come with me Mama*. But she didn't.

Aidie said she watched as her mom stood there at the threshold of the back door, frozen with freedom, until her father had leveled the shotgun and blew her face off. Now that she had to have someone wipe drool from her ever-open mouth and change her diapers, this was the one dignity Aidie could give her: to make her go out a martyr, a mother all the way.

But her mother didn't do that. And my mother cried viciously anytime I brought up my father. Even though she left him months before he died. Even though I'm the one who found him ten-to-twelve days dead.

Her mother, at least, left her in a more concrete way. Her father, at least, made it quick. But I, at least, have one fully dead and one fully living. That was enough to mean I should never complain, only understand.

Empathy. Jesus, how it can stretch and stretch and stretch when you love someone, how it can stretch until it's nothing but an unconvincing excuse and laying awake all night trying to tell yourself something that makes sense.

Aidie came out from the trees holding her bikini against her chest. Ike did not come out but there was rustling going the other way, deeper into the wild. I know, I know.

"Clem, can you tie me up?"

She presented her bare back for me. I looked, and then I grabbed the straps. It took a minute because my hands were numb. Aidie was patient though. She just stood there without complaint until I figured it out.

Then, she motioned for me to join her on the shore and drink another beer while she finished Ike's. Condensation cried between the fingers clasped around his beer. We sat there quietly getting a new level of drunk.

"Is he...?" But then I realized I didn't want to know.

"Not a little 'let,'" she said anyway, "but not a full boar neither. I'd never seen it before."

The sharp acid of bile flooded my mouth and I slipped my head between my knees in the sand. I did not vomit. My eyes went momentarily blind with tears —lacrimation, that's called —but I did not cry. I would not overflow.

My daddy'd told me I was but *a trapped man in the heart* and I intended to keep that true. I swallowed and swallowed, and then brought my head back up and the beer to my lips. Aidie didn't say anything. Aidie, I could see, was smiling in the dark.

Weeks passed and the days began to really start ticking down toward school. By August, I realized I wasn't going back. You could say I made the choice to drop out—and I did—but it was one of the only things that ever flashed with such certainty in my life.

I tried and tried to picture school and going back to sit in those carved-up desks and pass notes with normal girls while Mrs. Lees pretends to teach us about Dickensian England. I no longer read while Aidie took those men to her room; I laid flat out on the Florida Room floor with my eyes closed like some crooked yogi, desperately trying to see myself stepping back into that life again.

"Linoleum and bathroom stalls," I'd plead to myself. "Let me see chalkboard and PA systems. Lockers and bleachers. Anything, anything."

Nothing, of course. I thought for a minute that maybe I just couldn't really picture things at all, that maybe I'd all along possessed this defect and had never noticed and so this really didn't mean anything. That struck a flutter of hope for a minute. But then I tried to picture other future things—tried not to, really, but tried—and they all came so easy.

Drinking at Donna's: permadark room that shuts out the permabright days, expensive AC shocking the skin, glistening wood of a bar that stretched from the door to the bathroom, a chilled glass slid over that sways but never sloshes.

Cleaning up my dad's empty trailer to sell: stained carpet I'd have to rip up with my bare hands, counter-tops crusted with the brown of an abandoned place, the smell always lingering even after I've cleaned and painted and hung up thrifted posters and burnt every candle I've ever owned. A smell I would somehow get used to, or at least a smell that would slide into a familiarity like home.

Trying meth: Aidie and I standing out in the parking lot of Donna's with some boys long after dark, my feet making nervous pawings into the gravel when someone brings it out, the oversweet syrup clouds hitting my nose before anything else does, the unmis-takable *click* in my brain as something hits right and comes rushing out, the torture of one of those boys feeling so good but never good enough until only the sun comes and I'm left unbearably ill in some unknown one-bedroom.

Getting the fuck out of here: still unsteady in Clyde's now-unneeded car, wind screaming louder than the Sabbath tape, two types of hair flying all around me, trying to sing along to lyrics I can't quite make out because the road all looks the same and we cannot stop to rest until we get where I'm going. Slapping my hand against the wheel as I sing to ward off a sleep I don't want, gunning it a little faster, always a little faster, because I need out already.

Seeing the beach for the first time: too dark to really see by the time we're there but a moon hung like a decorative lamp in a sky stolen of stars, the end of a wave running to my feet with more strength than I'd ever given nature, water so cold I gasp when it finally touches me. A crab springing from beneath the wet sand and pinching me, me letting it.

I saw all this better than I could see yesterday. Then, because I guess I wanted to hurt myself even better, I tried seeing my father and I running into each other again at the grocery store, at the spring, at Donna's. I tried seeing him seeing me now, a little older, a startle in his eyes at his *little girlie* grown.

All I got was the yellow-pulsing black of my own eyelids. Same as school. So there was that.

I didn't go to the front office to formally withdraw from school. I agreed with Aidie that it *wasn't worth dealing with those old bitches* but really, really-really, I was too ashamed to show my face and say those words and sign those papers and give those women something to cluck about. It was cowardly, I could admit that, but it was easier to just let them count me among the dozens of empty chairs that take up more and more of the classroom with each grade.

Some teachers might be disappointed to find I was just like my mama after all, but I couldn't care about that. They could kiss my ass, I told myself. Graduating never did anyone I knew any good. I didn't need to start my life with any ceremony and papers telling me to do so. Aidie helped me to remember that.

When that Monday came and I felt my nerve falter, Aidie came to save me. I woke up cold that morning and realized Aidie wasn't in the bed. She was surprisingly warm, like a heating pad in my arms.

I sat up and looked at the clock: 5:30 AM, the same time I would be getting ready for school. A little pain pulsed through my fingers when I made the connection. I *would* have, I still could. If—

I sat there frozen with too many possibilities. Each minute that blinked by on the digital clock made my heart drop, but it also brought me closer to closing that door. If I were going to Honors English 4, I would have perhaps turned in a first-week poetry assignment with a line like: O the ease an ossified path brings!

But choicelessness comes with no small peace, at least for me. I think I could've been one of those happy housewives, high on prescription pills and safely secured within my pretty picket-fence prison, had that been an option for me.

For as long as I stayed laying in that bed, I hadn't yet made an option. I knew that once I got up, I would be making a final decision and I'd have to live with that forever. It didn't matter, none of it fucking mattered, but you can intellectually understand one thing and also recognize that a little part of you is always going to wonder, always going to hold regret like a boil between your toes, something you feel a little with each step and

"Oh, my darling Clementine," Aidie sang from

somewhere in the house. Her voice, a pretty one too, came under the door clear and strong as the breezes before a hurricane. "Dreadful sorry, Clem-en-tineeee…"

I got up, grabbed a shirt hanging on the doorknob, and pulled it over my head. I couldn't find shorts, but then I didn't bet that Jeff would be up at this hour so I risked going bottomless. I opened the door and followed the song out into the kitchen.

Aidie was rinsing out a big bowl at the sink. There was a pan on the stove, a carton of eggs and a plate of meat cut into thin rectangles on the counter, and four glasses on the table arranged two-and-two across from each other on the table. Two of the glasses were filled with what I guessed was orange juice; two of the glasses had a dark liquid like Coke. Aidie shut off the tap, turned around, and smiled.

"Wakey-wakey," she said, stepping into me to plant a kiss on the cheek, one that practically *smacked* as she pulled away like in the cartoons. She was all smiles this morning. She looked at me looking at the complete shock of her cooking and laughed.

"Eggs and bakey," she said. "I figured we could start the day with some substance, maybe go apply for jobs around town later. It's going to be a good day!"

Bacon. My eyes flicked back to the counter, to the plate. Who was it? It was something I couldn't wonder about, but did anyway.

I once joked that Aidie was like Tantalus when she sold sandwiches around town for gas money. She didn't know who Tantalus was and didn't seem to want to. And anyway, I knew what she was feeding me. I just trusted her not to feed me anyone I knew for any longer than a passing hello. Nobody I knew outside of her own room. Nobody I worked on with her.

The oil in the pan began to crackle and I flinched when she threw four pieces in with the force of a slap. You had to wait until the pan was *just about ready to burn before you throw 'em on because it's gotta all cook at once to cook good* and I trusted Aidie because she did a lot of things, yeah, but she did home-cooked meals best. All it took from her was a little nod in the direction of the table and I went to take my seat.

Eggs and bacon. Rum and Coke. Eight ounces of orange juice to wash it all down. Breakfast of champions. I ate methodically, like it was medicine. By the time we'd finished up—and Aidie'd coaxed me into a second mixed drink before sunrise—I didn't even remember what Monday it was.

I cleaned up while Aidie washed her hair before we got all dolled up to go into town. Our first stop turned out to be the last. When we walked into the diner after their breakfast lunch, Mr. *please girlies y'all can call me Clyde* McCee hired us on the spot.

We were given the blue polyester dresses with white polyester aprons and told to come back the next day at 6 AM. It was better than we could expect; we wouldn't make any better money elsewhere.

Aidie and I went giddy, skipping two blocks more to cajole the convenience store clerk to let us buy two loose beers. Then we turned back and walked home—our new uniforms carefully folded over our left forearms, a sweaty bottle clasped in our right hands. Aidie was the type to get physical when she was excited and she suddenly hip-checked me, which threw an arc of beer into the street.

"Bitch!" I laughed, and crashed into her in return, though I didn't do it nearly as hard back. She used her two free fingers of her beer hand to try and pull my top down. I play-ran to escape her clutches. Her sandals slapped against the sidewalk behind me, but I was far outpacing her. I was always faster, funny enough.

I twisted my head around to stick a bit tongue at her like, *I'm beating you.* But I knew where my tongue would be later, eventually. She always took us that way when we'd been day-drinking.

I looked back just in time to see the truck that had turned onto the street at the end of the block. I stopped. The truck stopped. Standing there slightly breathless, squinting against the sunlight to see, is when I realized: it was Mr. Mueller. My old history teacher.

"Um," I said, and Aidie came up behind me. She touched my elbow. She already knew.

"Miss Davis," Mr. Mueller said. He eyed the beer. I didn't hide it. No point now. "You should be in school."

"So should you," Aidie said through my hair.

"I'm getting lunch on my planning period," Mr. Mueller said. "But that's irrelevant. Why aren't you at school?"

He wasn't talking to Aidie. Aidie they'd already given up on. Aidie they expected. And that's why

Aidie didn't feel *no real way about it* today. He was looking right at me—and he looked almost hurt.

"I'm working now." My voice was no higher than the hush I'd use to talk to Aidie during some of his lessons. "I'm not…I'm not finishing."

"Oh." He sat back. "Oh. Are you sure about this? You could still come in tomorrow."

"No, I'm sure."

I very nearly said: "I'm sorry." But then Aidie was there.

"Well," he said, then coughed. "Well, I'm just surprised is all."

There it was: disappointment. I wasn't used to being on the other end of it. It bloomed in the pit of my chest like a dark flower, all spikes. My stomach ran cold as if it was filling with blood. This was my weakness above all weaknesses, one looming so large that I was always aware of it. There was no surprise of self-discovery; ever since I could remember, I would do anything to make people not think badly of me.

I wasn't sleep-walking through everything with Aidie, mind you—I fucking knew. I was just smart enough to understand the *why* of me, but I guess not smart or self-loving enough to figure out *how* to fix it. And the way Mr. Mueller was looking at me, I would have done just about anything to get him to stop.

Aidie spoke so suddenly it made me jump. "You could come over to our house and talk with Miss Clemmy about it. Or at least give us a ride home. S'hot out."

I turned my head just a fraction to catch a look back at Aidie. She was in her prime *fuckable brat* stance:

left hand on the hip, right hand shielding her eyes from the sun, a defiant squint while she looked him in the eye. Like I said, I was smart, or at least smart enough. But not enough to walk away.

Aidie squeezed between us in the truck. I prayed that maybe he wouldn't talk and he'd drive us home and that would be that, but he and Aidie were chatting by the time he'd pulled onto Main Street. Then I started praying he'd even switch to admonishing about *your potential to find a career over a job Miss Davis* but then Aidie's hand was on his thigh and he did not seem to mind. The next time I looked over again, he was brushing little circles from her knee to the hem of her skirt.

I still don't understand how she did it. There was magic, yes, but it wasn't like every single man turned out this way. Plenty of rides we got were perfectly fine. Almost as many men politely returned Aidie's bait with paternal care as the other men would pull out their dicks before we even got back to the house. It wasn't a possession so much as a pig call. And Mr. Mueller had pricked up his ears.

If there was anything I wanted to say, it was trapped in my throat. Aidie put me on the couch and stuck a drink in my hand. Mr. Mueller chose the spot next to me. Aidie flipped through records as she filled otherwise dead air with *whatever prelude bullshit they won't hear anyway so there's no need to be thinking so hard about it.*

He cleared his throat a few times. I pretended not to hear it. When he leaned over, his warm exhales tickled my earlobes and I could have gagged.

"Your mom?" It wasn't a question, but I nodded. "Your mom and I, we went to highschool together. Same school, of course. We weren't too close, but one time she got into a fight with her boyfriend at a party and kissed me to get back at him. She wanted to go to the bathroom together, you understand."

"..."

"We didn't, though. Rodrick—her boyfriend, not your father just yet—dragged her out and took her home before we could. She wasn't inebriated—drunk. She was just mad at him. They didn't break up until senior year."

If there was anything I wanted to say, it was trapped up in my throat. Globus sensation. My mouth could not open, my tongue could not move. Just as well. I had no idea how to respond. He took a sip of his drink and leaned back over.

"She used to be really pretty. Your dad was an asshole, excuse me, but he was smart. When you walked into my freshman class, I knew immediately that you were her daughter. And when you opened your mouth, I knew exactly who your father was."

His hand on my leg. His other arm thrown over my shoulders. That same *I'm fucking* smile I'd seen on so many men before.

I helped Aidie this time, more than I ever had before, but not fully. You understand. By the time that would have come, he already had. I herded him out with the gentle insistence I'd seen Aidie use with the rest of them.

"You see what I mean though, right?" Aidie asked me later. I'd been pacified by more beer in the backyard, gone hazy enough that I didn't even really mind Jeff hog-hunting within our sight. "You get it now?"

"I think I already did."

"Aw, baby," she laughed. "If you really did, half the state would be swarming by now."

I wanted to laugh. Instead I said, "Was that all to show me how many men are bad like that?"

"No." Her smile dripped with something. "I just wanted you to feel better about dropping out."

If I was as vicious as her, I could've returned with something about how Mr. Mueller had taught me so much and how now he'd left me with the ultimate lesson. Thanks to him, I did learn that I was just as capable as Aidie—whatever it was that let her do the things she did, I had it too.

The revelation brought conflict, that space in my chest oscillating between equal parts pride and terror, thrill and revulsion. I could mother monsters just like Aidie, but what control I had over it I did not know.

Too many questions: how did Aidie figure this out, do you have to hate the man to make him, do diseases and impregnation still apply, on and on and on. I could open my mouth and understand everything.

Instead I just nodded at the ground. And we kept drinking, drank until I couldn't even remember what had me so confused, drank until I wouldn't fully remember the rest of the day afterward. A gunshot made me scream at some point.

I woke up later with the imminent threat of vomiting, but I know I managed to untangle myself from Aidie and get poised in front of the toilet before it actually happened. I felt a hand rubbing my back and realized she'd follow me to the bathroom. And that's when I started crying.

"I'm a bad person," I think I said. "I deserve to die."

I don't know what she said back, if she said anything at all. I just remember her arms snaking around my chest, wiping my face, pulling me back to bed.

Morning—or afternoon, rather—came and every-thing was fine again, sleep remedying most of the ills yesterday had brought. We were extraordinarily late to our new job but Aidie managed to smooth it over and get Clyde to *train you with the dinner shift I suppose since y'all too pretty to turn away but you can't be fucking up like this again now.* By the end of the week, we were bringing home more money in tips than either of us had ever seen in our lives. Leaving started to become a real possibility.

The weeks began to slide again, colliding one Saturday into the other until it was already November and we got the faintest hint of a chill when we drove to the breakfast shift. It was nice, settling into that routine: up and at 'em before daylight, playing our sorta Southern accents up and down depending on the table, topping up little white mugs with hot black coffee, rushing our side work cutting lemons and sweeping the dining room when noon hits so we can get home as quick as we can to change into our swim-suits and go drink down at the spring, sometimes find a man, other times go home and cook dinner together. Jeff would pester us for a plate of his own, but he otherwise didn't really bother us beyond the looks and occasional *you know if you're taking all those men back maybe you could help me out one of these days.*

We went to bed early these days. Even on my most restless nights, Aidie would always get me to at least lay down by 11 PM. In the mornings she'd let me sleep while she took the first shower. She cared like that.

November, then. Any chill from the morning had always been well burned off by the time we were outside in the afternoons and on this one, we decided to lay out in the backyard instead of at the spring. I had a book I forgot to bring back to the library in my hands. Aidie sat with a ring of nail polishes around her. She was giving herself a manicure, letting them dry for at least an hour in the sun, and then she was going to do mine after. We were both too occupied to get good and drunk, for once.

It was maybe a mistake I didn't know we were making. I could've been numbed up and then everything could've been different. But for the first time in a while and then for a very long time after, I was sober. It's an irony I've never been able to quite articulate. Anyways.

I'm halfway through a particularly dense paragraph when Aidie softly calls, "Here piggy-piggy."

I look up to see a boar peeking out of the treeline, slowly coming out into the sun. He wasn't quite as big as the others I'd seen and his tail swished more like a dog. He seemed friendly even, like I could hold out my hand and he'd come to rub his head on it. Some wild things can be open to humans until time tells them differently.

Then it hit me: it was a juvenile. *Not a little 'let but*

not a full boar neither. And here he was, biggest he'll ever be.

"Hi, Ike," I whispered.

I swear to God, he lifted up his head and looked at me. He looked at me for the longest time. What if I could fix him? That hope was like a bomb in my chest. Every poison has an antidote, I think. If we had this terrible power of transformation, there could be a way back.

But there was no way back—not for Ike, not for Aidie, not for me. Only way to go was to keep wading through this shitswamp I'd put myself in. That's all there is: one foot dragging over the other in the muck, close your eyes at the worst parts to prevent nightmares, and hopefully find the shore. That's what I get.

A sound like a breeze and I looked over to see Aidie blowing on her nails, looking all the time at Ike. Ike did not move, except for his swishing tail. It was like he was waiting.

"Jeff," Aidie called out.

He came leering over behind us, the late afternoon sun throwing his shadow long across the grass. I didn't have to look to know he had the shotgun— same one his dad used, by the way.

"Come on now," Jeff said as he walked into the trees.

He clicked his teeth the way you'd call a pet. Ike blinked at me before turning around to heed Jeff's call, following after him at a trot. I went inside and threw up in the kitchen sink, then dipped my head under the faucet to drink until I threw up again. When I looked outside, Aidie was flipping through my book.

It really starts here, I guess. Other, ordinary criminals would be talking about mitigating factors leading up to what they did. All this was mine, more or less. I never excused it in my head or tried to justify what I did. I had no judge to convict me, no God to be forgiven by. I only had Aidie, but that was always enough. And maybe I just needed her to only have me.

I was drunk that day, of course. The day that happened a couple weeks after Ike did. For once Aidie was out alone to *get us some groceries and get me some fancy spice rubs* and I just couldn't find the energy to get off the bed until after she left. I had moved to the living room to watch TV when Jeff came and sat next to me. He was home—a lot—but this was one of the first times we'd been alone together and he wasn't holed up in his room. His hair was wet from a recent shower. I could even smell cologne.

It was what it was, and it wasn't anything that had to be said. But only I knew, you know. He was ignorant until the end. I'm sure you can connect the pieces that I'm too cowardly to paint.

Aidie. Aidie had me impressed. She figured it out within an hour and when she asked me, she sounded almost amused. I had the shotgun on the coffee table ready to go. I expected her to shoot me. She didn't. She just asked me to straighten up the kitchen after she made dinner. And when the clock hit 11, she asked me to *come get some shut-eye already*.

I fell asleep fast, thinking maybe she was calculated and was going to smother me in my sleep. But I woke up the next day, and the day after that. So. Back through the shitswamp.

It was after the holidays but before I found out when Jeff came back. Aidie saw him first. She brought me from the bedroom into the backyard, then went back in to get the shotgun. I knew it'd only be fair for her to make me watch, but instead she put the long gun in my arms like a sleeping infant.

"It's time," she said, and kissed me on the cheek. "You can do it."

And you know what? I could.

I BLEED WOMAN

The girl sits, waiting, on the edge of her bed. The bed is high off the ground, some sort of dorm standard. It's high enough that to get on it, she has to boost herself up from a footstool she bought just for this purpose. It's high and narrow. She has to sleep straight and with her arms tucked in. It's a bed built to prevent sex, is what it is.

She thinks briefly of the first night when she fell, this new elevation and new lack of width something she never thought she'd grow so used to. She finds it so normal now, how high up she is sitting. When the doctor comes out of the bathroom and over to her, to his one-time patient, they are nearly level with each other.

"Are you comfortable?" he asks, but they both know it doesn't really matter.

"I'm not uncomfortable," she offers. The doctor manages a tight smile.

"Well."

He gestures towards her own desk. The papers he insisted on are neatly laid out for her. The girl gets a flip in her stomach—the kind they all had talked about right before getting it done—as she slides herself off of the bed and searches for a pen.

The doctor, ever the professional, produces one from his coat pocket. Dark blue, not black. Her English professor would've thrown a fit. She almost wants to laugh as she throws hasty loops across the signature lines.

"That takes care of everything?"

The girl hands the stack to him. He nods and slips them into his briefcase.

"Would you like to go in first?"

The girl has to squeeze past him in this little hallway to get in. Her bathroom—heart-shaped night-light, pink hand soap, vanilla candles—hasn't much changed. The polka dot curtain is drawn back to expose the scrubbed bath, saran wrap covers the tiled floor. The scalpel, his one instrument, lays neatly across her side of the counter.

"I have to ask again," he says from the door.

"I know."

"This is what you want to do?"

The girl turns around. She is quick to note how hard the doctor tries to hide his disgust for her, for all of them, but it's useless information. She would be, too. But she can't help herself from saying:

"God, the way my roommate looked after…"

She doesn't mean to bite her lip. His eyes flare. He probably hates her, he probably can't wait to get it over with so he can take her money and run the fuck away from another little freak.

She confirms, "Yes, I really want this."

"Ok." She knows he's already had enough of her. She knows he must have had enough of all of them. The first must have been enough, and the money can't be all that good. There's something that must compel him—beyond his own hate, beyond his own disgust—to do it. And that makes her even more excited.

He vaguely waves toward the tub. "Go ahead and…"

The girl knows. She'll never admit how many times she's practiced taking her necklace off and kneeling over the tub. And this time, when it really counts, she does it with the grace of a condemned queen. She hopes the doctor notices.

And maybe he does. From her position, she can't tell. But she feels his eyes on her. It won't be much longer.

"One last time."

He has to make her say it. She thinks, perhaps, he wants her to say it, he likes to make her say it. Maybe this is the part that keeps him going procedure after procedure, girl after girl.

She could ask him if he does—if he likes it—but even this far in, she's a bit too shy for that. So she just guesses that it's what he wants out of her, and she tries to make this last word something he will really like.

"Yes, doctor."

It comes out almost breathy, like a moan. She didn't mean it that much.

She hears him come in, hears him pick it up from the counter. He bends over her close enough for her shoulders to feel the brush of his weight. The girl has never been so near a man before.

With this last minute, she thinks—hopes—that the doctor will be thinking about her later. In the car, driving home. In the kitchen, chopping some meat for dinner. In bed. Maybe he loves her, in his own private way. He at least cares enough to be here, now, with his hand resting oh-so-gently on her shoulder, reaching up to oh-so-lovingly hold back her head.

He loves her, she decides. In these last seconds, she

can pretend that he's performing the ultimate act of love for her. It is a big favor, after all. That has to count for something. And when he draws the scalpel across her throat, she can almost believe that it was something loving.

LYING TO STRANGERS AS ART AND OCCUPATION

Today she was going to be a wife. Yes, that was what she decided on—she'd tell the summer tourists stretched out on the shore that they were newlyweds, sweet young newlyweds who needed gas money to get home from a honeymoon gone bad. That could go well, really well even. Newlyweds could attract a great deal of sympathetic donations.

Would she be pregnant? No, that may offend good taste. An aspiring mother, perhaps. She could make them see it in her bright little eyes. Every last piece of change to spirit two nice people back to Minnesota or Ohio (depending on what hometown team blanket they were laying on) to start a wholesome little family and put this blip of a predicament behind them.

It'd be better than yesterday. Yesterday she told people her boyfriend had ditched her in their motel room, leaving her broke and desperate through no fault of her own. Three hours to get $50 and a few pitiful glances, but more often came the head-shaking and insults. She couldn't stand the insults. Telling her she's a leech, scum. A slut who deserves this. Like she didn't already know.

She told him the plan as they sat on the edge of their open van and waited for the beach to fill. By noon, it was clotted with cars and the gleaming skin of people who don't often see the sun. A veritable sea of fish for them.

They'd go together. They'd look best going together. And they'd dress nice enough and use what was left of her concealer to cover up the raw skin around their nostrils. She used the very last remnants on her fingers to dap under their bloodshot eyes. It was an investment they had to make—if people caught even a whiff of how they sometimes took a break from this life, they would never get a cent.

He clipped her only nice piece of jewelry—a beaded necklace she couldn't help but hand over a crumpled five for at a fair—around her thin neck. Some days it's best to make their chronic poverty apparent, but today called for looking only temporarily lacking of funds. Her cheap cover-up, his thin band shirt. They did their best with it.

And she was right. $127 *for getting back home, kids.* She hid the biggest bill in her bra, a twenty from an older lady dressed completely in the crisp, bright seaside wear that people with summer homes here get at the outlets. It worked. It fucking worked.

He said they ought to go out for dinner. He said they deserved a small luxury. She was instantly annoyed. How could they? But then it wasn't like they had many expenses. Or that they would ever be able to save up enough to change, either.

And sometimes, with those big portions and limitless coffee and complimentary jellies at a greasy spoon, it could work out to be cheaper than getting a few items at the grocery store. She pretended to be delighted by his offer, even if it was their money he was taking her out on.

He saw right through her, though. He knew what she thought and he knew she was right: he was a loser and he brought her into a loser life. That unbeatable fact colored everything he ever did, throwing a regretful wash of Predator Purple or Son-of-a-Bitch Blue over even the nicest gestures.

Of course all he wanted to do was give the love of his life everything the world had to offer. Really. But he was too much of a coward to do what was best for her, which would be to slip away while she's sleeping in the van and call her parents.

What he would do—which was the best he could do, anyhow—was to give her a surprise he'd been saving for a night like this: a bottle of conditioner he managed to steal from a drugstore down the street. It was hard doing that, especially without the cover of his upper-middle-class girl with him, but he had managed to get a bottle of her favorite kind in his pants and out the door before the new kid at the register knew the difference.

He'd wrap it nice in yesterday's newspapers to make it look like a real present even, a Santa Claus of the necessities. She'd be excited, really excited. They hadn't had conditioner in probably a month.

Funny how so many things they once thought were essential—contacts and closed-toe shoes and cold creams—they had had to forsake and, to their total surprise, had managed to survive without. They could still be presentable in a beach town with their salty hair and dirty-burned skin. Anywhere else and they'd be looked at. But not here, not in their parameters.

They used what was left before they went out and, bad as it was and bad as they were, it's what let them be most in love. Passing them on the street—her skipping and twirling ahead to the restaurant, him calling out after her—one wouldn't be faulted for mistaking them for a pair of carefree trust fund vagabonds.

But that's the kicker: they weren't. They'd been living out of a broken-down van by the sea, far removed from any relatives or friends, for nearly a year. It'd been a cross-country trip that ended where the vehicle did. Going nowhere fast, as they say.

The 24/7 diner that they hadn't already run up trouble in. Big Help Wanted sign plastered on the hostess stand. Desperate enough for extra hands that they might even hire them. She straightened up his hair in the bathroom and pushed him into the manager.

He was so happy to get two young people looking for honest work that he comped their meals. No interview. Come back in the morning, 7 AM. A new shirt for him to work the dishpit, a clean-pressed apron for her to help wait tables.

They aired out their very best clothes, their Sunday clothes, out in the windy dark as they washed up in the waves. Too many thoughts, too hopeful, swirled. They didn't dare speak them, as if it would jinx them from being real. But she knew and he knew and that was certainly enough.

And they knew what they'd be tomorrow.

SLIPS

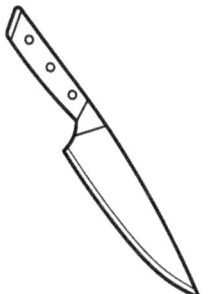

Closing on Sundays meant closing with *her*, so this was also the night that closing always managed to stretch one, two hours after he'd turned the lights off outside. He'd waved off her offers to do more than the dishes. He liked her in movement—the shake of her ponytail as she banged out coffee grounds into the trash, the way she danced around to wipe down tables—but to see her in a lull was a thrill that, here, felt faultless.

It started with her, that Sunday. They wrapping up with dishes in the cafe's kitchen / pantry, which wasn't too much bigger than the one in his own apartment. It made for a snug fit, the two of them at the sink. The Closed sign had been officially turned over an hour ago. She started.

"I might get my nose pierced."

After they'd said everything they needed to get closing done, that's how they would pass rest of the night. Idle chatter that went nowhere. Sixty-something Sundays in, and he was still trying to figure out how to make it go somewhere.

"That'd be cute," he dared.

He wiped syrup bottles on the rack behind her, wondering if he would actually like that change. "Of course, not here."

"Right." The back of her head bobbed. "Not here."

"You could do it on a vacation though?" he offered. "That way, it'll heal up while you're gone and then you can have it out at work. Caleb takes his tongue ring out before each shift."

"It'd need more time," she said. "I'll need to wait—"

"Huh?"

She took sudden interest in the grime on a kitchen knife.

"You putting in time off?"

"....."

The jump between the quiet and conclusion came quick.

"You quitting?

"...."

"Hey," he said, "you quitting?"

She only squealed and pulled both of her hands out of the sink. Her mistake was the common one kids always commit: she'd let the knife trip down and slice deep into the meat of her thumb. A guilty thought flashed—*you dumb bitch*—as he watched the site whiten before the appearance of steady blood moved him to action.

He wrapped the wound with the rag he'd had in his hand. Of all the times he'd thought about touching her, he'd try out her response—a virginal smile, a twitch of surprise, a true youth's blush. This was the justified contact of manager with an employee, right, but he was still almost disappointed at the absence of electricity. Spark apart, she was shocked still.

"Pressure," he said, though he was the one doing it. "Pressure, pressure."

"I'm not...it doesn't hurt." she said. Red was creeping fast across dirty-white, and he grabbed another rag to cover it. "It's not good, right? It's not good that it doesn't hurt?"

He wrapped it again and pushed her arm above her head.

"Hurt over heart," he said, "thumbs-up."

"It's a lot." She wasn't being dramatic. Red was starting to show again.

"Hang on a second?" His eyes flicked to the office. "I've got my phone in there…."

With her a-okay hand, she produced one from her pocket. He decided she was well aware that phones were supposed to stay in their lockers and just took it.

"Passcode?" he asked, then, "Who do I call?"

"911?" Blood was falling. He forgot to tell her to keep keeping pressure when he took his hand off. He forgot girls her age never knew to do anything for themselves. A drop smacked her nose and made a slide towards her mouth. "Right?"

He held the phone. She watched him. He put the phone down. He tried something.

"Why don't I just drive you?" She blew blood off of her lip. "I mean, if it's that bad."

It took him a second to see that she was crying.

"I don't wanna get in the car with you."

She even took a step back from him. His instinct went to close the distance. She stepped back again.

"Please."

"What's—"

"I'm not getting in the car with you." Her face had gotten pale, and she was still trying to get away. "I'm not getting in the car with you."

COOKIE DEATH

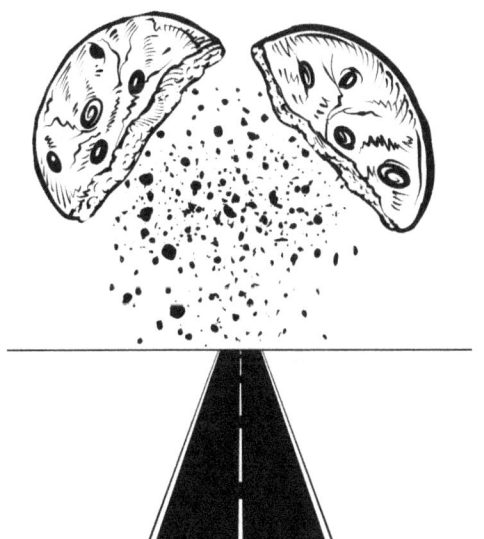

H eather was printing up the check for her last table when the GM put his hand on her shoulder. At first she didn't flinch, didn't even turn around.

"They're closing now and I'll go cash out with Randy in a minute," she said. "I wasn't rushing them."

He took the still-warm check off the printer and passed it to the hostess before she could do anything. The hostess, a high-schooler she trained last week, dropped the check off to the man.

But the woman paid. Heather calculated she'd probably get a 15% tip, ending the Breakfast–Lunch shift at maybe $75 before the hostess got her cut. Wonderful.

"Heather," the GM said, "let's go to the back office."

She wasn't getting fired. She could've snorted, thinking about what they'd do without her. She only took this shit shift as a favor for the FOH key. They called her out of bed this morning to come.

Someone had probably done something, and she needed to watch security tapes with him again. Repeat dine-and-dashers, newbie servers not charging their friends, cooks selling drugs out of the walk-in— what'd she witness this time?

This time, there was a cop in the back office. Three people in there made for a tight fit, but the GM gestured for her to sit down and shut the door behind them anyways. The cop didn't say anything.

There'd been some incidents before—they got hit overnight a couple years ago, accidentally hired a sex offender, even a murder in the parking lot. There had to be some new drama. Heather was already thinking about how many people would try to prod her for gossip and how she'd fend them off. Part of why she would always have a job here is because she kept a tight lip.

"You can step out," the cop said.

But not to her—the GM. He did. The cop then finally looked at her.

He introduced himself as Officer Harnet. He was a young guy, maybe 25. He reminded Heather of the kid who worked grill she once overheard call her a MILF. She still got a kick of how he couldn't look her in the eye. This guy couldn't either.

"Ma'am," he said.

Heather was 39. He stopped, then started again.

"I'm here because I need to inform you of an automobile accident that happened about a few hours ago in Tallahassee. It involved your daughter."

"Oh."

"She unfortunately suffered serious injuries. She… ma'am, I am so sorry, she was pronounced deceased. The coroner is currently on the scene."

"Like…on the road?"

"Um." He wiped sweat from his forehead. "Yes, where it happened. Going southbound down North Monroe. Not far from Lake Ella. Are you familiar?"

Heather shook her head. Shook her head. She'd only been there to help Jane move into her dorm, out of her dorm, and then into her apartment this summer.

They were quick turnarounds—the four hours up, the few hours there, and then right back on the road for the four hours back. Jane insisted there was never anything worth sticking around for, and Heather had always thought that correct. She'd always felt better driving away from that shitty little town—even if it meant driving away from her daughter, too.

She had enough time to grab the little trash can under the manager's desk before she suddenly retched. The cop threw up his hands and pushed back on his feet to roll his chair away from hers. Then, with an awkward amount of distance between them, he reached over to pat her shoulder. He produced a travel pack of tissues from his jacket and handed it to her. Heather took one and wiped her mouth with it.

"Do you need some water?" he asked.

She couldn't make that decision right now. Several people would ask her that throughout the next few days.

"Is Jane still out there?" she asked. "Is my daughter still in her car? Was it her car?"

He didn't have many answers for her. All the information he knew had already been said. He was only there to notify her and relay the coroner's request for her to come identify the body tomorrow morning. The body.

The cop left and the GM came in. He cashed her out quickly. She tried to hand over her hostess's cut, but he just waved her away. Her last table had left a $100 tip. Nobody talked to her on her way out. Instead of leaving through the back, she went up front so she could give the hostess $20. The girl, Alena, started crying when she did that.

"Have a good day," Heather said, surprised to hear it come out so softly. Her throat burned.

She went home, took a shower, and changed into a hoodie and leggings. She didn't realize it used to be Jane's hoodie until she'd already put it on. They'd shared so many clothes it was hard to keep track. She packed an overnight bag and got in the car.

There was no fear—as long as no one else was hurt, Heather would've loved to die on impact in some smashup, so quick and brainless that she wouldn't even remember existing and would never have to really start contemplating a Jane-less life. Still, she knew she was going to drive carefully.

Heather stopped at the closest gas station to top up her tank and buy a Monster. When she'd gotten on the highway, she resumed playing her Spotify and dropped it into the empty Big Gulp in her cup holder. That was her stereo.

Jane used that trick in her car, too. They both drove old beaters inherited from Heather's great-aunt. No stereos, no AC most of the time. But, free. But—oh my god—probably not the safest. She could imagine Jane's little sedan crumpling from practically nothing—

She became disoriented by the four voices that suddenly filled her car. It took her maybe two minutes to realize nobody else was in there with her—it was the podcast she started playing on her drive to work this morning. She'd been trying to wean off her true crime addiction and start listening to those self-help shows her friends kept talking about. The whole Bad Bitch, Icon, Girl Boss, Slay Queen shit that made her feel a little old. Heather dared to look at her phone just long enough to change it to a serial about Jane Toppan. There's a real Bad Bitch right there.

It was almost midnight when Heather made it to the off-campus motel. A man wandering in the parking lot said something to her as she walked to the lobby, and she just growled at him.

"Weird bitch," he said, and she growled again.

Still, she pushed the room's chair against the door after she locked it before kicking her bag under the bed and then laying on top of the sheets. The people in the next room were having an argument loud enough to make out about half of the words. Heather shut her eyes and when she opened them again, light was already blaring in through the big front window.

* * *

They did not let her see the face. Instead, they asked Heather to identify her via a picture of her wrist. They wanted her to indicate a tattoo there. Heather didn't know about the tattoo. But that was Jane's wrist.

Apparently, she'd decided to get *STOP* inked on the baby-delicate skin there. It was ugly, block-y, prison-looking letters like the tattoo her ex had gotten on Jane's third birthday. He'd used her money to pay his friend $80 for the job, $20 for each word. Heather wondered if Jane did it herself. Her tattoo, that was.

That wasn't enough for them. The two men—a cop and maybe the coroner, she already forgot their intro-ductions—went to a corner of the room to confer with each other. The man in slacks briefly stepped out and said something to someone on the other side of the door. They again offered her coffee. She again declined.

There was a knock at the door and the man in slacks answered it. Someone in the hallway passed a paper to him. He thanked whoever was there, shut the door, and then gently placed it face-down on the table. Heather flipped it over and leaned in.

"What am I looking at here?" she asked.

For a second neither of them answered. The slacked man cleared his throat.

"That is a picture of a scar on the right side of the decedent's face," he said.

Suddenly Heather could see it—the half-inch little line that ran from the corner of Jane's nose to just below her eye. She'd been cut by a rock that flew out of a truck she'd been tagging too close to on her bicycle when she was 12. The ER bill had been $1,200. Heather was on a payment plan until Jane hit high school for that one.

The photo had been taken so tight that Heather almost wouldn't have known it was her baby's face if he hadn't said so. She looked for the freckle that folded into Jane's face when she smiled. She noticed instead how it didn't even really look like skin, much less Jane's. It looked like evidence, a picture that should be on *Dateline* or something. She pushed it away from her.

Three times she indicated that it was Jane. Two times she again said that she did not want any coffee. If they had offered tea—or fuck it, even gin—she would have taken it. Coffee, especially the cheap hot coffee they'd almost certainly serve in a Styrofoam cup, would make her shit. That's the last thing she wanted to do, at least here.

They didn't immediately offer to show her the body, and she didn't insist on viewing it. It. There was no need to see any more of the green-gray skin shown in the photo. They'd said something about "extensive damage" too, and Heather didn't want to know anything about that. No viewing, no wake, no question for open or closed casket. When they asked, Heather answered: "Cremation, please."

They weren't religious. Jane hadn't said much about anything like this, but she'd been scared shitless by the resurrection Biblical bullshit her paternal grandmother had told her the few times Heather let her babysit. Even last month, Jane changed the zombie movie playing on TV.

So she'd be cremated, Heather guessed. It seemed the better of the two options presented to her. If she had the money, fuck, she'd turn Jane into a diamond or something. Or build a big funeral pyre in the middle of nowhere so she could jump into the fire and burn along with her.

Jane would be transported to a funeral home in Midtown (Midtown?) and they'd cremate her this afternoon. Heather could have a small ceremony—a celebration of life, they called it—if she wanted, but the next available date would be the day after tomorrow. It'd give her time to get friends and family up was what they had mentioned, but there was nobody to call.

Three out of four grandparents were dead and Jane chose to cut contact with Jason's mother. Heather was going to honor that. Jason was…wherever he was. His siblings were wherever they were too. Friends, classmates, maybe even some ex girlfriend who'd want closure—Heather couldn't think of anyone close enough for that. She couldn't think of anyone.

Nobody else had died in the accident. The cause of death—asphyxiation. Apparently Jane was already close when she lost control. They'd found a cookie lodged in her throat.

"What kind of cookie?"

They couldn't say.

Jane couldn't keep steering and shot onto the sidewalk. A tree tore through the front of the car. That was about all Heather could remember. It was too much information at once.

There were groceries in the backseat that they let Heather have. The car itself was going to the junkyard. They removed the other "effects," as they called it, before towing it away. Everything—minus Jane—was handed to her in clear plastic bags. She got her keys in a manila envelope marked "JP WF 20 2/10/19." Someone had to help her carry everything to her car.

Heather had requested six copies of the death certificate. They said she'd need it. She did—one to end Jane's lease, another to "withdraw" (which seemed like an inappropriate word for it) her from the university, and a third to send to the financial aid office. She couldn't be released from rent, tuition, and loans if Heather didn't prove what'd happened.

There would be no news articles she could submit instead, and that was preferable. The only hope Heather had was that Jane didn't end up in some Wiki list. It was a headline waiting to happen: COOKIE DEATH. If Heather ever saw it, she'd take an arms class just to shoot herself. She promised herself that much.

A representative from the funeral home offered to help her file an insurance claim. Insurance? The only policy Heather had was on herself, Jane as the beneficiary. She'd need to cancel it soon.

The representative said that their (private and piece of shit) health insurance might reimburse her for cremation costs. For now though, she'd have to pay out of pocket. $342 due now. She put it on her credit card.

The three other copies would be kept with all of their other documents at home. In case there was anything else, in case anyone else needed to know. Heather had Jane's birth certificate, every police report she'd filed against Jason, both of their high school diplomas, and her own parents' death certificates in a folder under her bed. This was their family history, more or less.

All that was left was to pack up Jane's studio apartment. Her landlord told Heather that she could stay there through the week, if she wanted to. She didn't. She was driving back the second she was done. They would ship the ashes to her via certified mail. Heather already knew how it'd come to her—in a sealed plastic bag inside a cardboard box. Jane had used her threadbare tote bags on that last grocery trip. All the waste on her account…she would've been appalled.

The smell hit Heather as soon as she opened the door. She couldn't even step inside. She walked to the bodega behind the complex, bought some menthol rub to put up her nostrils, and came back. Her nose burned, but it was bearable. She went in.

Food everywhere—ice cream melted on the stove, a still-wrapped TV dinner in the microwave, bagels rotted on the counter, unidentifiable pastry crumbs in the unmade bed. Vomit clogged in every drain. Tied-up shopping bags lined up against the wall by the door.

Heather picked one up. It was heavy, the weight of whatever making it sag toward the ground. She squeezed the contents. It felt like dough, maybe mushier. She undid the tight knot and looked in. Chewed food. She tied the bag up again and put it back down.

There was a scale in the space between the fridge and the dishwasher. A long piece of paper was taped at eye-level above it. It was a list of numbers written in purple, then pink, then a light blue ink.

119.2

119.6

118.4

116.8 LOW

117.4

117

117.6

116.8

122.4 FUCK

120.2

119.4

120.6

125.2

128.4

124.2

137.8 PIG

135.4

140.2

138.8

The trashcan was filled with whole slices of bread, an unopened pint of ice cream, loose chips, and what looked like an incorrupt pan of brownies. It also reeked of bleach. Heather had to drag the entire can and tip it directly into the dumpster out back. Hopefully no raccoons would get into the bag. Such waste.

Heather used the rest of the trash bags under the kitchen sink to pack Jane's clothes. She was taking everything home. She braced herself to find something embarrassing hidden in her underwear drawer—a weed pipe, condoms, maybe even a vibrator—but there was nothing. Jane's secrets had been in plain view.

The only clean place left to sit was the floor. Heather could feel the cold vinyl through her leggings. This scene seemed like that of a stranger's. She would've paid for a therapist, she swore. But she couldn't say for sure.

"Oh my love," she said to the walls, to the mess, to nothing in particular. "I didn't know you'd been hurting like this."

Then she got back up and kept cleaning. There was still so much to do.

SLAUGHTER

F ather said it'd be messy, yes, but Seer still couldn't have known what he meant until it was over. She could squeeze the blood from her overalls if she really wanted to. Blood peeked from between her fingers every time she closed her hands. Messy, messy, messy work. But that's what it means to be self-reliant —when you live like this, you're responsible for everything it takes to get the food on your plate, killing and all.

Not that anyone was eating tonight, of course. Such a waste. Feathers were glued to the barn walls with blood and white shit that had splattered everywhere. Yep would have to go spray it down later, once he was done hosing people off. If he didn't get to before it dried, Seer knew she'd end up scrubbing the walls alongside him.

So much work. So much mess. So much waste.

Waste was the very thing Father had gotten them all rallied against. The false wide world out there lived in it—too many people committing too many evils to make too much money to buy too much stuff that none of them even really wanted. On the Farm, excess was never an issue. They extracted exactly what they needed from the ground and their animals to sustain themselves. Nothing more, nothing less.

They all got a bit skinny, sure, but their bodies were *strong*. Every boy, girl, and little child at the Farm were ready for whatever came their way. And nobody was starving—really, nobody was ever wanting for anything. Father made sure of that.

But Father, for all he was, could not have foreseen

the CIA poisoning their flocks and fields. It was a terrible discovery. He'd gone out that sunrise just as the agents were all running off, their crimes revealed in the early morning light. Seer couldn't imagine how hard it must have been for him to announce it during Morning Call, to look on as all the girlies wept and he couldn't do anything about it. His strength constantly amazed her.

It was a good thing, at least, that Father was the first one out there that morning, since none of them would ever have seen what had happened until it was too late. Everything, everything looked as it should have. Crops all seemed fine. Chickens and cows were just as they'd always been. Sky blue as ever. They would have all died within the day if it weren't for Father. This was not the first time Father had saved them.

Still, to be saved means work. Hard, horrible work, work that makes you scream until you hiccup later on when you're finally alone. Since it was all tainted, the fields had to be burnt. The boys did that under Father's careful hand. To save their animals from a drawn-out death, they had to be killed right away.

Seer couldn't even watch when a chicken was slaughtered for Friday dinners. Father knew this was one of her Purifying trials and assigned her to the task. She couldn't, of course, argue. She could only follow him in alongside everyone else and pray for it to be quick once he shut the door behind them.

There were three ten-pound bags of dry rice in the pantry and a case of canned lentils buried behind the house. This would perhaps last them two weeks, three if they really made it stretch. They'd have to. Father would pray and find their new path in the meantime. He would. He'd have to.

Times were getting tough, Seer had to admit that. But it was never supposed to be easy. To be saved means work.

Christ was persecuted by the government. The saints all suffered at Waco, at Jonestown, at Spahn Ranch. To be saved means work. They must suffer persecution, too. It was simply their turn. As Father always said, that was the ultimate path. Suffering to salvation.

As Seer waited for her turn to have the blood hosed off her body in the barn, she was sure Father would figure things out. She never worried, and she certainly wouldn't worry now. Now, all she wondered was whether Yep would hurry up. There was so much to do, and it was already getting dark.

She wasn't being very good. Annoyance was an evil thought and rushing wasn't what they did. It was time to practice patience, she supposed. She stretched her legs out on the ground and leaned back on her elbows.

It'd be her turn soon enough.

LIVE NOW

H e only had notifications enabled to see when she was live. It was an organic show to the core, free of schedules and programming. It happened when it happened, and he had come to structure his days so that he'd always be ready for it: *totallyhonest222 LIVE NOW*.

And for however long she'd stay on, he'd take her with him—to the kitchen, the bathroom, back to the desk in his bedroom, and on and on. He could do everything but sleep while watching her, and sometimes he'd even crack a Monster to stay up with her when she was on one of her marathons. One time she mentioned how late it was—3:28 AM, the same three numbers on the top center of his phone—so he knew she was in the same time zone, knew she was also suffering the same manic night. He came to see a lot of similarities between themselves.

His phone flashed just as he pulled into the parking garage. He'd gone on what had to be the last 7/11 cigarette run until his unemployment hit again. It was late of course, but not unacceptably so. He encountered a number of cars on the road and had to nod at another customer inside. The night was still very much young. And the show had begun.

He kept the phone raised to eye level as he navigated, half-blinded by the screen, out of his car and back into his apartment. Her voice blared through the empty hallway. With the odd hours he kept, he usually didn't run into any stranger-neighbors walking the short stretch to his doorstep.

Sometimes he did, though, and they would wince

at the words coming from the speaker he held to his ear. Those passing-bys had never embarrassed him into buying headphones. Nothing could at this point. With the way everything ended up for him, that—embarrassment, shame, the sense of being perceived and being perceived badly—wasn't even in the periphery of his mind.

And when you have something like her in front of you, the little things tend to slip away anyhow. He was above it now. She—Alice—helped him rise above, really. Really.

There were some semipressing biological matters—a quick meal, a glass of water to keep his kidneys from complaining, an inevitable shit—that he'd have to attend to at some point tonight, but for now they could wait. As his ass found its way back into the grooves of his desk chair and he synced his phone to the bigger of his two monitors, he guaranteed himself the first ten minutes to be watched without interruption.

And it seemed like good timing, too. She'd mostly been out of view, pacing the background as she *set the vibe* and even leaving at one point to retrieve a bottle of whiskey. She drank Southern Comfort mostly, but she'd often say that she would go for something better if she could afford it. Those comments usually brought a fire of tips, but never from him. He didn't approve of her drinking. But she was back, and she'd poured herself a glass, and it was on. He settled in.

"For all of you little incels just joining now," she said, "well—okay, not *all* of you are incels, I'm not taking shots at *all* of you—how many are on here right now, anyway?"

She brought her face close and narrowed her eyes into a near scowl. "226, okay, not so bad. I'm just saying, a lot of you are probably jerking off right now and I'm not even going to bother telling every single fucker joining in that just because I'm not going to put anything nice on for y'all, I'm *not* getting naked! There are a million other streams popping off right now for that shit. If you wanna see a girl shoving a stapler up her ass, go take your tips over there. I don't give a fuck."

She always gave this disclaimer in the first hour of her streams, but it never stopped the comments coming in.

show us titties mommy
6664538291 Alice text me anytime I will pay
I dont want see you naked anyway bitch
let me join your live pls?

She didn't bother with mods. She believed in free speech above all, and just ignored the haters and spammers until they went away. It usually didn't take too long for them to drop out of the stream. Her apathy was the greatest punishment any viewer could suffer, and that cold lack of reaction casted them back to the cumcams and 4Chan pretty quickly.

He really couldn't think of anything worse than being ignored by her, to have a comment go completely unnoticed and for her to simply squint and carry on. He didn't think he could actually handle it. That's why he never left a comment.

"User43-fucking-whatever," she said after another sip, "you've sent like a dozen fucking roses already, don't you have a girl to send real ones too?...yeah, that's what I thought. I guess I'm all you got, huh?...any girls in here tonight? Where my lezzies at? I don't know why else you'd be watching…SlyGuyxx—dumb fucking name— no I'm not going to rate your cock, ew. You guys need to stop fucking asking me dumb fucking questions."

Of course, just set it off:

Rate me cock?Rate my cock princess plsi've spent $15 on you already and i'll spend $30 for cock rate pleasealice my alice id do anything to get you to laugh at my little dickrate cock plscock rate plspls rate cockcockrate

He was perhaps a little disappointed when, finally, she gave in.

"Okay, fuck, whatever. I'll pick one I see in my inbox and rate it later. I want to talk about something else right now."

That seemed to placate the chat, at least for the moment. She picked her drink up, swirled it around. He took a swig of his Monster. She set her drink down. He tipped one rose. The ka-ching brought her back.

"I want to talk to you, my loving losers, about something very important. Something topical. Something more important than anything else you'll hear today, probably even this month. Are you listening? All of you?"

Someone sent a Super Heart, an animated filter that briefly flew into and covered the screen with a fluttery SMACK that might as well've been a FUCK YOU. Her face, when the animated heart had finally cleared, was frightfully still. Calm before the storm.

"WHAT THE FUCK!" She screamed, her voice rising in pitch to almost that of a little girl.

Was that what her tantrums had sounded like? How could she be so loud in what looked like an apartment? The cops never seemed to show, for all the yelling she did. She screamed again, and then her voice smoothed.

"Seriously, fu-u-uck you-u-u. You had me yelling like white trash, yes you did! Who was it?...JimMurphy74, you old fucking man, I bet I can find you right now."

She turned to a laptop out of view and was mostly quiet for the next five minutes. He used that time—still with the phone in his hand, of course—for a bathroom break and to grab a paper plate of (somewhat dry but still passable) lunch meat. He was almost finished eating when she suddenly grabbed the phone and flipped her camera around.

"See!" It took a minute for the glare of the bright screen to focus on her big reveal: the Facebook profile of old, bald, pudgy Jim Murphy from Ohio. She rapped a short, red-chipped middle nail against his digital head.

"There you are, Jim Murphy, I fucking see you, yess-s I do. And you know what I'm gonna do? I'm gonna send a screenshot of all the Super Hearts, roses, and eggplants you've sent me to your wife. Except I already did, yes I did! And now I think I'm going to post it on your wall, that's right. Because you disrespected me, you really did! So you need to be fucking taught a lesson your mother seemed to have forgotten —r-e-s-p-e-c-t, respect, right. What do y'all think? Did your mothers teach you better than poor old Jim Murphy?"

I'll always listen when you speak baby
U taught me good mommy
Jim doesn't live too far from me Alice, I can go and teach
him a lesson for you. From, Alvin of Akron OH. ;)
simps get wrecked lol

As for Jim, there was no response. JimMurphy74 had already left the stream.

He was tempted to use his other monitor to go check the guy's Facebook, but that would break a rule —no dividing of his attention. When Alice was on, he watched, and he watched without interruption. He'd try to remember to check later. Of course, the poor dumb bastard would probably take his public profiles down by then. They usually went completely dark the same night they were struck.

He always had this odd urge to go check in on them, the latest victims of her volatility. Sometimes he could tell exactly when and what would set her off— just like that Super Heart, that was obvious. But sometimes she'd catch him by surprise.

Sometimes he thought even she was taken aback by her own swings, the times when her eyes seemed to widen at herself while her mouth carried out an attack. Alice, brown-blonde Alice, Alice of the awesome impossible power to destroy any man online, Alice perhaps couldn't always help herself. But he knew he could just as well be committing a bit of wishful thinking.

"Well, his life is about to get interesting for once. Anyw-a-y-s. What was I saying?" She paused, swishing what was left of the whiskey in her glass.

He thought maybe the stream had briefly lagged when her arm suddenly swung—the movement looked too quick not to have been a glitch—but it was only when he heard the crash offscreen did he realize she had thrown her drink. Her scream caused the audio to flatten. This was Alice unveiled, the Alice who could blow out 434 speakers around the world. He did not turn it down. He'd only had one complaint this year and could take another. And with the erection unfurling like a hot comma of shame in his lap, he deserved the entirety of the triple-digit decibels she was bringing to his ears.

"He fucked me up! All y'all fucked me up!" She grabbed the phone and pointed it at the wet spot on the carpet where her glass lay somehow still rightside-up. "You think I like wasting shit? A drop of this gutrot is worth more than all of you little jerkoffs! He threw me off. He fucking threw me off, and now I don't want to talk anymore."

Her voice caught like she was choking back a sob. He'd never seen (though of course if it would happen, her being hidden behind the camera makes sense) or heard her cry before. In the 2.14 years he'd been watching, she'd never been on the verge of tears before. Something in his stomach stirred, his dick (still abominably upright) prickled. He opened the chat and, carefully, plucked the keyboard.

You will never understand the space you take in so many souls.

HIGHLIGHT+CONTROL CLICK+DELETE

This vulnerability is so beautiful.

HIGHLIGHT+CONTROL CLICK+DELETE

On my big brother's grave, I have never gotten off to you. Anyone who has probably does it at church too.

HIGHLIGHT+CONTROL CLICK+DELETE

I love you.

DELETEDELETEDELETEDELETEDELETEDELET-EDELETEDELETEDELETEDELETEDELETE

Then he settled.

What were you going to say?

It was meaningless, really, a stupid question that would be lost amongst the sea of comments, and she was calming down anyway. She walked back to her desk, repositioned the phone, and adjusted herself in the screen. She was reading. Perhaps she was pacified by the hundreds of men begging to be forgiven, perhaps she was only planning. But she was quiet.

"What was I going to say?" He felt his heart drop out of his ass, felt it falling all four floors into A144's master bedroom, felt it laying there a dark-red mess with fibers of the cheap white-gray carpet sticking to it. She was speaking about him, to him. He had her attention.

"User684blah-blah-blah, I see you lurking in my streams all the time. Why don't you tell me what I was going to say?"

Was this heartbreak? The pain crashing against him like a rogue wave, he knew he deserved it. He did not comment. He would never make that mistake again.

"You know what? Nobody gets anything else from me tonight. Try again tomorrow."

His reflection looked back in the now-black screen. *totallyhonest222 LIVE ENDED.* The night was over. There was nothing left to do but go to bed and let sleep reset the reality he found himself in right now, a reality where Alice was angry with him. He was wrong in more than one way—there was, after all, a worse death than her indifference.

Try again tomorrow.

* * *

Except tomorrow didn't offer a second chance, and neither did the next day or the day after that. Each day he waited for *totallyhonest222 LIVE NOW*, for his phone to go off and for his stomach to flood with an almost acidic relief, and each day got nothing but ghost vibrations in his back pocket. Alice had always been vocal about never taking action against the viewers who pissed her off, but was it possible he had angered her enough to break the no-block rule? Could he have been banished like that?

He could still see her account and its status: *Active 4 days ago.* He made new accounts to double-check every time that number rose. *Active 5 days ago. Active 6 days ago. Active 7-8-9-10*—at some point, it just felt like self-flagellation. She was gone, and it was his fault, and she may never come back.

What had he done that was really so bad? Out of all the viewers, what had it been about him? He had only ever admired Alice, went without cigarettes whenever he felt anything more than a brotherly love toward her. He never even spoke her sacred name out loud. Alice, Alice everafter, Alice of all evils. If this was what she decided would be, then he had to only understand that he deserved it.

Her absence dragged into weeks, then months. The weather cooled into jacket territory. Pumpkins and orange wreaths began to appear on his neighbor's doors. A letter from the property manager appeared on his. He was not welcome to renew his lease there. He had sixty days from the time he read their notice to find somewhere new to live.

He spent at least twenty of them laying on the floor of what was supposed to be a living room (he had never bothered with furnishing this part—what'd he need a couch and TV for?). During that time, suicide seemed like a viable plan, only he couldn't get himself up to do it. He had maybe enough energy to resituate himself in the bathtub and blow his brains out if he had a gun, which he did not. He knew that anyone who worked at Armed World would see him as tomorrow's next mass shooter, and he didn't have the money for gun shows. Other methods were of course free, but took too much planning to execute. That's about as far as he went with that.

So, life. So, new apartment. He was at least lucky they weren't evicting him; a black mark like that would mean the literal streets. But on a fixed income in the age of hyperinflation, he was still fucked—just not so completely fucked that he still had to try.

One night, he forced himself to his desk and turned on his computer. When he opened a new browser, it automatically redirected to her profile. It had been almost half a year since Alice last appeared and this felt too much like some step away from her. Then again, hadn't she been the one to—

No. He would not think about her like that. Whatever she did, she did it with just cause. She had her reasons. And he? Only a futon, three Monsters, a box of frozen Smuckers, one last loose cigarette, some mouthwash, a desk, two monitors, and an ever-pressing notice to vacate. And if he wasn't going to take the time to research easy OTC overdose combos, he may as well try to find somewhere to go.

Filtered by his budget, the available listings thinned down to only three pages. He found a 1/1 only twenty minutes away with a bathtub instead of a shower stall, a requirement for him. He clicked through the floor plan and model photos. Even their best photos of a staged apartment didn't conceal the worn carpet and chipped paint on the doorways.

The carpet.

A light beige, which could be in any complex. But the way the room led into a master bathroom with a sliding door to a closet on the right—it was the same setup as Alice's bedroom. The same backdrop to her rants and ramblings all these years. Despite his best efforts to minimize hope, a possibility too bright to be his own began to open up. If life didn't quite feel worth living, it at least felt livable now.

Rent for the 1/1 increased before he could go sign the papers, so he had to downgrade to one of their studio units. Which was fine with him, really. He had promised himself he'd never live in just one little room ever again, but what was the extra space other than empty anyways? A studio admittedly suited his small life best. Anything more was simply pride, and he had no use for it.

It took two cartrips to move from one place to the other, and that was only because his futon took up the entire backseat. "Home" changed in under an hour. He knew this had to be the right decision because of how easily his reality shifted that day, how much better this reality already was. Even the promise of proximity to Alice was enough. This was enough.

Of course he was a realist and of course he knew that Alice might not actually be there. There could be another complex just like this one in their time zone states away; even if there wasn't and this was really the belly of the beast, she might have moved out of here months ago. But he never entertained these ideas as anything more than obligatory comedowns to hold back his hopes. Whenever he got into it with the Christians in high school and they said, "I know God is real because I can just feel Him," he would call them morons.

Now though, he got it, and he almost felt bad. As sure as the Jesus freaks felt their god's glow, he felt that Alice was near. That he would see her in the flesh was as much of a fact to him as his own heartbeat. It was just a matter of when.

Weeks of fluttering over a potential run-in, of fake-outs of faraway brunettes in the parking lot and female screaming through the walls, left him impatient, and this is when he made a fatal mistake. He decided to try speeding up fate and began roaming the halls at all hours of the day.

He devised a method—he used a randomizer app to draw a number between 1 and 12 and choose AM or PM. This would be the time he woke up the next day. Then he used the same app to pick a letter between A and G, and then a number between 1 through 5. This would determine which building and what floor he would start on. Then, he would simply work his way up or down the building and around the complex, then repeat the pattern until he either could not physically hold in a piss any longer, or went dizzy with hunger, or couldn't hold up his eyelids. Often it was all three at once, but it took hours and hours before that happened. And he'd always walk himself right to that edge.

He listened to four entire podcasts series and lost enough weight to warrant a new pair of jeans within two months. These markers felt almost like progress. But incidental byproducts of his search did not bring him any closer to Alice. Only his own persistence and the brutality of chance would find her. Time—lots of it —was all he could ever really give. So for as long as he still had it, he would continue his rounds through the complex.

Of course the day came. He was halfway through Episode 108 of his latest podcast (something about My Lai) when up ahead he saw the light brown hair, the long shirt over leggings, the scowl. His brain made the connection just as his feet almost gave out. He stopped. She kept going, then passed him. He turned around and, carefully, followed.

B261. That's where she went. Now he knew. Now he could be prepared.

Next time didn't have to be some rushed run-in caught in the hallway. To come face-to-face with fate couldn't be taken that lightly. He had to be perfect. He had to plan. And when he finally bridged the 1,122 feet between them, he would do it so gracefully that she'd forget he had ever wronged her. It just had to be right. He would make it right. Even if it cost every-thing, he'd make it right.

* * *

His daily million-mile walks reduced to down two floors, across to the building next to his, up one floor, and through four hallways. B261. She didn't have a Ring, but he couldn't hang around her door in stasis all day, in case of neighbors. So he did very slow circles around that floor, round and round. Round and round.

Every time he passed B261, he imagined himself kneeling before a cross to pray she'd open the door. B261. Could he be that lucky? Could he be that lucky now? Could he be that lucky later? B261. He bristled at the sound of a knob—any knob—turning. Maybe on the next round, maybe the one after that. But it would certainly come. He was encircling the very heart of the queen's lair. Sooner or later she had to come out. And he'd be ready for her.

That was his pride, though, an illusion of control. He wasn't the master of anything, and reality revealed herself in the worst ways whenever he forgot this fact. Their meeting, finally, did not happen as he was passing her door; it happened as he was walking back to his own apartment with all the damage of a long day spent lurking: a sour mouth from dehydration, eyes blinking a beat too slow, a brain that didn't piece together who was stomping toward him. It only made sense when she collided her fist into his collarbone.

The pain bloomed hard, racing from the point of impact out to his shoulders and down his spine. When the floor suddenly seemed too close he thought he was falling, but then bile erupted from his mouth and he realized he bent over to throw up. He could hardly take in anything other than the throbbing heat coming from his clavicle. It was undoubtedly broken.

A little sandaled foot with grown-out black polish stepped into his field of vision. He forced himself to stand up straight and steadied against the wall behind him. He raised his head, then lowered it a bit. She was shorter than he thought.

"I haven't called the cops," she said. "Yet."

"The cops?" This was all wrong already. His voice wasn't much more than a whisper.

"Are you fucking stupid?" She almost smiled. "Yes, cops are called on stalkers."

"I'm not," he said, then stopped. It sounded ridiculous before it even left his mouth.

"How'd you get my address?" she asked.

"I didn't."

"Alright, then I'm done here." She turned around and strode off.

This is the point where the hero would shout "WAIT!" and have an explanation that set everything right, but he could only groan until she came back. It took him a full minute to catch his breath and say:

"I recognized the layout online. I had to move. I moved here. I just wanted to talk to you."

"About what?" She wasn't shouting. She didn't even seem that upset. She just looked at him, and she looked a bit scared. How old was she, really? The little thing before him couldn't be more than 20 after all.

"I had asked what you were saying that night."

"What?"

"In the chat. I was the one who had asked what you were going to say. And then you logged off and never came on again. Why?"

She stood there just breathing, her chest rising up and down. He tried not to feel the beats of pain each time he inhaled.

"I was just done." She offered nothing else. Her

answer hung heavy in the air before sinking to the ground between them, the weight of it unbearable and definitive.

He expected her to shrug, but she didn't. Instead she said, "If I see you in my building again I will kill you. I own two guns and I always carry."

He already believed her, but she pulled a small black pistol out of her purse to show him anyway. The bottom (barrel?) was bedazzled with pink rhinestones. She put it away and stepped back.

"Do you understand?" All he could do was nod.

"Okay." she said, nodding as if to herself. "Good. Because I'm done, and I don't want any of you to look at me anymore."

Of all the imagined conversations and all the ways he thought their meeting would go, this reality seemed as impossible and unexplored as the idea of them making love. He slumped further against the wall. There was nothing he could say to make her forgive him, to maybe make her really take notice and understand him. Everything had already fallen apart.

Just before she left, she said, "My name isn't even Alice, by the way. I made her up."

Or maybe she said "I made *it* up," but she was down the hall before the words made sense. The semantics didn't muddle the message: that Alice had only ever been a mask she could slip on and off for an audience. Alice could've been anybody, could be anybody. Alice was now officially unowned, cast aside for some other life that didn't include him. Alice had never been so within reach.

He stood there a minute gathering strength, willing

himself enough adrenaline to make it through his threshold. No help would come should he collapse. He counted backwards from three and forced himself forward on one, the momentum swinging him each step until he almost fell into the door. He shook the key into the doorknob until he felt the lock give and then made it inside, finally landing on the futon. Everything hurt, but he would live.

A broken collarbone, according to the Internet, couldn't really be treated beyond maybe a shoulder brace and some pills. The bone couldn't be set to heal in a cast; he just had to wait out the pain and try not to hurt it any worse in the meantime. He would go out and buy booze when he could. Even a big bottle of vodka would be cheaper than a pointless ER bill, and would probably work better than anything they'd prescribe him, too. This was the first and hopefully only time he'd ever concede to self-medication.

So this was how he'd put himself back together: sleep, a shot when he woke up, a wipedown to stave off smell, a one-armed clothes-change, another shot, a meal out of whatever he had left, kill time on the computer, another shot, sleep, repeat.

There was something to be said here about a caterpillar in a cocoon, and he tried to imagine himself working his way into being a butterfly, but that just didn't quite work for him. He knew he was changing, though. Some transformation had been undergone and after so many shots and sleeps, he would emerge from the stink of unwashed skin and indoor cigarettes reborn, made anew in the pain and into someone else entirely. Another shot, another sleep. He'd never be himself ever again.

* * *

Alice picked at the bra band that had dug too deeply into its ribcage, an unfamiliar pressure it still had some getting used to. Alice was not yet fully Alice; the superficial things happened seemingly overnight, but the rest was stuck in the purgatory of an in-between. The hair had grown some but still necessitated a wig for showtimes, while the body would need pulling-in and padding-out indefinitely. All the other markers of Alice were easy enough, though—nail polish that was always painted over without using remover first, bangles sliding up and down its arms in an unbeautiful music, makeup to smooth over the original's uncertain masculine features and bring forth a sharp look of femininity.

The face needed work, but not so much to look beautiful as to embody the anger of Alice. The mannerisms weren't quite there yet. The dismissive *pfft* out of clenched teeth, a bored scan of the comments, the ever-present threat of a smirk from the corners of the mouth. These were difficult to master, but eventually they would be done. It knew that there would come a day where that way of movement, at present so foreign and forced, would come as fluidly as water running down its newly-shaved skin. It would all come just as Alice eventually.

It practiced bringing down the eyebrows (which stung from a recent plucking session and glowed red under concealer) while flaring the nostrils just a touch. This was Alice's default face, so it best learn this one most of all. The mechanics were right but something in the eyes wasn't quite convincing. But as always, give it time.

It relaxed and leaned back from the mirror. Wig, Southern Comfort, take a seat at the computer. It teased out a feeling like readiness and knew that was enough to go live.

And it was *it* in its head because to be *she* didn't feel any more correct now than *he* did anymore. *They* didn't make much sense either, though logically this would probably be most apt. But *it* just felt right. *It* was the closest thing to being unreal it could get. It felt like an *it* the way an angel or an entity was. It never felt all that human—boy, girl, or otherwise—to begin with. And it didn't matter. Now, it was simply Alice.

It breathed in, out, in, and opened the app. Alice was just a little off-center in the frame and visually not quite complete, but this was the closest to a resurrection these fucks would get. It hit GO and felt some unseen hand grip its stomach while across the world, thousands of men received a notification from a long-missed (and easily acquired) account: *totallyhonest222 LIVE NOW*. One, then two, then four, then just two again filtered in. It kept quiet and watched the count by the red eye. Two, six, fourteen, thirty-two. At 226 it finally spoke.

"Welcome back, my little losers," Alice said. "It's time we finally talk. I have something important to say."

ACKNOWLEDGMENTS

Mona, Dad, Mom, Max, Aunt Meg, Gramma, Papa, Jenny, Gabby, Tia Adri, Susu, Alaan, Zak, Jamal.

Veronica, Avery, Kelly, Madeline, Calista, Aaron, Brian, Alyssa, Alain, Randy, Brandon, Jon, Edmond, Manny, Chuck P.

Ethel Cain, Pierce the Veil, Reverend Kristin Michael Hayter, Dolly Parton, Elyanna, Subtronics, BB King, Nick Shoulders, Queens of the Stone Age, Rett Madison, Billie Holiday, Kali Uchis, Iggy Pop, Saint Levant, Blind Willie Johnson, Skrillex, Gorillaz.

John Waters, Chuck Palahniuk, Alyssa Nutting, JT LeRoy, Kristen Arnett, Flannery O'Connor, Toni Morrison, Augustina Bazterrica, Stephen Graham Jones, Mona Awad, Johanna Sinisalo, Kurt Vonnegut, more.

Camren Camren Camren.

PREVIOUSLY PUBLISHED

"Adam and Eve in Quarantine" first appeared in *Eclecta* and later in *Redemption*.

"When vanity is otherwise the poor girl's only virtue." has appeared in *The Showbear Family Circus* and *The Short Place*.

"Monroe and Mansfield at a Picnic" and "Damned in D3" first appeared in *Thought Thinkers*.

"Finding Siren" first appeared in *The Short Place*.

A portion of "Triptych of the Interworld Girls" first appeared in *Eclecta* and later was published in full in *Redemption*.

"Skeezy Geezer" was featured in *Redemption* and in *She'll Get There*.

The following stories first appeared in *Redemption*: "I Bleed Woman"; "Thoughts from one of those girl-types that disappear."; "Consort, 1953–1958"; "Cookie Death"; "Slaughter"; "Slips"; "The Seamstress and Her Sinner"; "LIVE NOW".

ABOUT THE AUTHOR

Zoe is a writer, fiber artist, beadworker, and enthusiast of North American folk art. This is her fourth book and second short story collection. She lives in Florida with her husband and more cats than she'll admit to. If you'd like to stay updated on all new projects, please follow @zoerose0 on Instagram or find her on Medium and Substack.

 instagram.com/zoerose0

REQUEST FOR THE READER

If you enjoyed this collection, please consider leaving a review on Amazon or Goodreads. Your review especially helps independent authors gain visibility and find more readers online. Thank you for reading.

ALSO BY ZOE ROSE

Who mothered the corpse?

She is found by a hunter one Sunday morning.
She lays, as though asleep, on the forest floor.
She has no name, but she had four mothers.

In a world where the dead are used without qualms by the living, the body of a beautiful young girl is claimed by four women: a witch, an artist, a whore, and a chef. Each allege to be her mother, and each have their own posthumous plans for her. Which woman will get to fulfill her desires? Who mothered the corpse? With the true possessor in question, a trial commences.

She'll Get There: Stories that no longer hurt.

In this story collection, the reader encounters four women—Clara, Marta, Georgia, and Lala—with difficult pasts and uncertain futures. Faced with real-life bogeymen, death, and unrequited loves, each woman must reckon with what has been done and choose what will happen to her. Zero's debut story collection weaves together real-life experiences to create a complex portrait of victims, witnesses, survivors, and aggressors alike.

Body Spells

This is a poetry collection of works written under duress and drama between 2018 and 2022. As the poet underwent the isolation of college, an ensuing (and expected) episode of depression, and a thankfully short bout with eating disorders, she sometimes opened a Google Doc and typed. *Body Spells* is the culmination of grief, grandiosity, and growth.

AVAILABLE ON AMAZON